A beautiful duchess, a lush, a pretty girl at the Princeton-Dartmouth Rugby game, a lowboy, a hill town and a mountain pass are a few of the people, places, and things that Mr. Cheever hopes to exorcise from his subsequent work by describing their lives, their triumphs and shortcomings. "In order to become readable again," says Mr. Cheever, "to say nothing of recouping some of its lost importance, fiction can no longer operate as a sixth-rate boardinghouse. And in a world that changes more swiftly than we can perceive—where even the mountains seem to shift in the space of a night— the process of eviction, of selecting characters of stature, can be as interesting as the final cast." In a sense, then, these libelous and compassionate stories are a series of envoys to people and situations whose claim on our attention is intense but not (Mr. Cheever hopes) final.

SOME PEOPLE,
PLACES, AND THINGS
THAT WILL NOT APPEAR
IN MY NEXT NOVEL

SOME PEOPLE, PLACES, AND THINGS THAT WILL NOT APPEAR IN MY NEXT NOVEL

by John Cheever

Short Story Index Reprint Series

BOOKS FOR LIBRARIES PRESS
FREEPORT, NEW YORK

Reprinted 1970 by arrangement with
Harper & Row, Publishers, Inc.

"The Death of Justina," "Brimmer," and
"Boy in Rome" first appeared in *Esquire.*
"The Lowboy," "The Duchess," "The Scarlet
Moving Van," "The Golden Age," "The
Wrysons," and "A Miscellany of Characters
That Will Not Appear" (under the title
"Some People, Places, and Things That
Will Not Appear in My Next Novel") first
appeared in *The New Yorker.*

STANDARD BOOK NUMBER:

8369-3449-0

LIBRARY OF CONGRESS CATALOG CARD NUMBER:

79-116947

PRINTED IN THE UNITED STATES OF AMERICA

CONTENTS

SOME PEOPLE,
PLACES, AND THINGS
THAT WILL NOT APPEAR
IN MY NEXT NOVEL

THE DEATH OF JUSTINA

So HELP ME GOD IT GETS MORE AND MORE PREPOS-terous, it corresponds less and less to what I remember and what I expect as if the force of life were centrifu-gal and threw one further and further away from one's purest memories and ambitions; and I can barely recall the old house where I was raised, where in midwinter Parma violets bloomed in a cold frame near the kitchen door, and down the long corridor, past the seven views of Rome—up two steps and down three—one entered the library where all the books were in order, the lamps were bright, where there was a fire and a dozen bottles of good bourbon locked in a cabinet with a veneer like tortoise shell whose silver key my father wore on his watch chain. Fiction is art and art is the triumph over chaos (no less) and we can accomplish this only by the most vigilant exercise of choice, but in a world that changes more swiftly than we can perceive there is always the danger that our powers of selection will be mistaken and that the vision we serve will come to nothing. We admire decency and we despise death but even the mountains seem to shift in the space of a night and perhaps the exhibitionist at the corner of Chestnut and Elm streets is more significant than the lovely woman with a bar of sunlight in her hair, putting a fresh piece of cuttlebone in the nightingale's cage. Just let me give you one example of chaos and if you disbelieve me look honestly into your own past and see if you can't find a comparable experience. . . .

On Saturday the doctor told me to stop smoking and drinking and I did. I won't go into the commonplace symptoms of withdrawal but I would like to point out that, standing at my window in the evening, watching the brilliant afterlight and the spread of darkness, I felt, through the lack of these humble stimulants, the force of some primitive memory in which the coming of night

with its stars and its moon was apocalyptic. I thought
suddenly of the neglected graves of my three brothers
on the mountainside and that death is a loneliness much
crueler than any loneliness hinted at in life. The soul
(I thought) does not leave the body but lingers with it
through every degrading stage of decomposition and neglect, through heat, through cold, through the long winter nights when no one comes with a wreath or a plant
and no one says a prayer. This unpleasant premonition
was followed by anxiety. We were going out for dinner
and I thought that the oil burner would explode in our
absence and burn the house. The cook would get drunk
and attack my daughter with a carving knife or my wife
and I would be killed in a collision on the main high-
way, leaving our children bewildered orphans with nothing in life to look forward to but sadness. I was able to
observe, along with these foolish and terrifying anxieties,
a definite impairment of my discretionary poles. I felt as
if I were being lowered by ropes into the atmosphere of
my childhood. I told my wife—when she passed through
the living room—that I had stopped smoking and drinking but she didn't seem to care and who would reward
me for my privations? Who cared about the bitter taste
in my mouth and that my head seemed to be leaving my
shoulders? It seemed to me that men had honored one
another with medals, statuary, and cups for much less

3

and that abstinence is a social matter. When I abstain from sin it is more often a fear of scandal than a private resolve to improve on the purity of my heart, but here was a call for abstinence without the worldly enforcement of society, and death is not the threat that scandal is. When it was time for us to go out I was so light-headed that I had to ask my wife to drive the car. On Sunday I sneaked seven cigarettes in various hiding places and drank two Martinis in the downstairs coat closet. At breakfast on Monday my English muffin stared up at me from the plate. I mean I *saw* a face there in the rough, toasted surface. The moment of recognition was fleeting, but it was deep, and I wondered who it had been. Was it a friend, an aunt, a sailor, a ski instructor, a bartender, or a conductor on a train? The smile faded off the muffin but it had been there for a second—the sense of a person, a life, a pure force of gentleness and censure—and I am convinced that the muffin had contained the presence of some spirit. As you can see, I was nervous.

On Monday my wife's old cousin, Justina, came to visit her. Justina was a lively guest although she must have been crowding eighty. On Tuesday my wife gave her a lunch party. The last guest left at three and a few minutes later Cousin Justina, sitting on the living-room sofa with a glass of good brandy, breathed her last. My wife called me at the office and I said that I would be right out. I was clearing my desk when my boss, Mac-Pherson, came in.

"Spare me a minute," he asked. "I've been bird dogging all over the place, trying to track you down. Pierce had to leave early and I want you to write the last Elixircol commercial."

"Oh, I can't, Mac," I said. "My wife just called. Cousin Justina is dead."

"You write that commercial," he said. His smile was satanic. "Pierce had to leave early because his grandmother fell off a stepladder."

Now I don't like fictional accounts of office life. It seems to me that if you're going to write fiction you should write about mountain climbing and tempests at sea, and I will go over my predicament with MacPherson briefly, aggravated as it was by his refusal to respect and honor the death of dear old Justina. It was like Mac-Pherson. It was a good example of the way I've been treated. He is, I might say, a tall, splendidly groomed man of about sixty who changes his shirt three times a day, romances his secretary every afternoon between two and two-thirty and makes the habit of continuously chewing gum seem hygienic and elegant. I write his speeches for him and it has not been a happy arrangement for me. If the speeches are successful MacPherson takes all the credit. I can see that his presence, his tailor and his fine voice are all a part of the performance but it makes me angry never to be given credit for what was said. On the other hand if the speeches are unsuccessful—if his presence and his voice can't carry the hour—his threatening and sarcastic manner is surgical and I am obliged to contain myself in the role of a man who can do no good in spite of the piles of congratulatory mail that my eloquence sometimes brings in. I must pretend—I must, like an actor, study and improve on my pretension—to have nothing to do with his triumphs, and I must bow my head gracefully in shame when we have both failed. I am forced to appear grateful for injuries, to lie, to smile falsely and to play out a role as inane and as unrelated to the facts as a minor prince in an operetta, but if I speak the truth it will be my wife and my children who will pay in hardships for my outspokenness. Now he refused to respect or even to admit the solemn fact of a death in our family and if I couldn't rebel it seemed as if I could at least hint at it.

The commercial he wanted me to write was for a tonic called Elixircol and was to be spoken on television by an actress who was neither young nor beautiful but who had an appearance of ready abandon and who was anyhow the mistress of one of the sponsor's uncles. *Are you growing old?* I wrote. *Are you falling out of love with your image in the looking glass? Does your face in the morning seem rucked and seamed with alcoholic and sexual excesses and does the rest of you appear to be a grayish-pink lump, covered all over with brindle hair? Walking in the autumn woods do you feel that a subtle distance has come between you and the smell of wood smoke? Have you drafted your obituary? Are you easily winded? Do you wear a girdle? Is your sense of smell fading, is your interest in gardening waning, is your fear of heights increasing, and are your sexual drives as ravening and intense as ever and does your wife look more and more to you like a stranger with sunken cheeks who has wandered into your bedroom by mistake? If this or any of this is true you need Elixircol, the true juice of youth. The small economy size (business with the bottle) costs seventy-five dollars and the giant family bottle comes at two hundred and fifty. It's a lot of scratch, God knows, but these are inflationary times and who can put a price on youth? If you don't have the cash borrow it from your neighborhood loan shark or hold up the local bank. The odds are three to one that with a ten-cent water pistol and a slip of paper you can shake ten thousand out of any fainthearted teller. Everybody's doing it. (Music up and out.)* I sent this in to MacPherson via Ralphie, the messenger boy, and took the 4:16 home, traveling through a landscape of utter desolation.

7

Now my journey is a digression and has no real connection to Justina's death but what followed could only have happened in my country and in my time and since I was an American traveling across an American landscape the trip may be part of the sum. There are some Americans who, although their fathers emigrated from the Old World three centuries ago, never seem to have quite completed the voyage and I am one of these. I stand, figuratively, with one wet foot on Plymouth Rock, looking with some delicacy, not into a formidable and challenging wilderness but onto a half-finished civilization embracing glass towers, oil derricks, suburban continents and abandoned movie houses and wondering why, in this most prosperous, equitable, and accomplished world—where even the cleaning women practice the Chopin preludes in their spare time—everyone should seem to be so disappointed.

At Proxmire Manor I was the only passenger to get off the random, meandering and profitless local that carried its shabby lights off into the dusk like some game-legged watchman or beadle making his appointed rounds. I went around to the front of the station to wait for my wife and to enjoy the traveler's fine sense of crisis. Above me on the hill were my home and the homes of my friends, all lighted and smelling of fragrant wood smoke like the temples in a sacred grove, dedicated to monogamy, feckless childhood, and domestic bliss but so like a dream that I felt the lack of viscera with much more than poignance—the absence of that inner dynamism we respond to in some European landscapes. In short, I was disappointed. It was my country, my beloved country, and there have been mornings when I could have kissed the earth that covers its many provinces and states. There was a hint of bliss; romantic and domestic bliss. I seemed to hear the jinglebells of the sleigh that would carry me to grandmother's house although in fact grandmother spent the last years of her life working as a hostess on an ocean liner and was lost in the tragic sinking of the S.S. *Lorelei* and I was responding to a memory that I had not experienced. But the hill of light rose like an answer to some primitive dream of homecoming. On one of the highest lawns I saw the remains of a snowman who still smoked a pipe and wore a scarf and a cap but whose form was wasting away and whose anthracite eyes stared out at the view with terrifying bitterness. I sensed some disappointing greenness of spirit in the scene although I knew in my bones, no less, how like yesterday it was that my father left the Old World to found a new; and I thought of the forces that had brought stamina to the image: the cruel towns of Calabria with their cruel princes, the badlands northwest of Dublin, ghettos, despots, whorehouses, bread lines, the graves of

9

children, intolerable hunger, corruption, persecution, and despair had generated these faint and mellow lights and wasn't it all a part of the great migration that is the life of man?

My wife's cheeks were wet with tears when I kissed her. She was distressed, of course, and really quite sad. She had been attached to Justina. She drove me home, where Justina was still sitting on the sofa. I would like to spare you the unpleasant details but I will say that both her mouth and her eyes were wide open. I went into the pantry to telephone Dr. Hunter. His line was busy. I poured myself a drink—the first since Sunday— and lighted a cigarette. When I called the doctor again he answered and I told him what had happened. "Well, I'm awfully sorry to hear about it, Moses," he said. "I can't get over until after six and there isn't much that I can do. This sort of thing has come up before and I'll tell you all I know. You see, you live in Zone B—two-acre lots, no commercial enterprises and so forth. A couple of years ago some stranger bought the old Plewett Mansion and it turned out that he was planning to operate it as a funeral home. We didn't have any zoning provision at the time that would protect us and one was rushed through the village council at midnight and they overdid it. It seems that you not only can't have a funeral home in Zone B—you can't bury anything there and you can't die there. Of course it's absurd, but we all make mistakes, don't we? Now there are two things you can do. I've had to deal with this before. You can take the old lady and put her into the car and drive her over to Chestnut Street, where Zone C begins. The boundary is just beyond the traffic light by the high school. As soon as you get her over to Zone C, it's all right. You can just say she died in the car. You can do that or if this seems distasteful you can call the mayor and ask him to make an exception to the zoning laws. But I can't write you out a death certificate until you get her out of that neighborhood and of course no undertaker will touch her until you get a death certificate."

"I don't understand," I said, and I didn't, but then the possibility that there was some truth in what he had just told me broke against me or over me like a wave, exciting mostly indignation. "I've never heard such a lot of damned foolishness in my life," I said. "Do you mean to tell me that I can't die in one neighborhood and that I can't fall in love in another and that I can't eat . . ."

"Listen. Calm down, Moses. I'm not telling you anything but the facts and I have a lot of patients waiting. I don't have the time to listen to you fulminate. If you want to move her, call me as soon as you get her over to the traffic light. Otherwise, I'd advise you to get in touch with the mayor or someone on the village council." He cut the connection. I was outraged but this did not change the fact that Justina was still sitting on the sofa. I poured a fresh drink and lit another cigarette.

Justina seemed to be waiting for me and to be changing from an inert into a demanding figure. I tried to imagine carrying her out to the station wagon but I couldn't complete the task in my imagination and I was sure that I couldn't complete it in fact. I then called the mayor but this position in our village is mostly honorary and as I might have known he was in his New York law office and was not expected home until seven. I could cover her, I thought, that would be a decent thing to do, and I went up the back stairs to the linen closet and got a sheet. It was getting dark when I came back into the living room but this was no merciful twilight. Dusk seemed to be playing directly into her hands and she gained power and stature with the dark. I covered her with a sheet and turned on a lamp at the other end of the room but the rectitude of the place with its old furniture, flowers, paintings, etc., was demolished by her monumental shape. The next thing to worry about was the children, who would be home in a few minutes. Their knowledge of death, excepting their dreams and intuitions of which I know nothing, is zero and the bold figure in the parlor was bound to be traumatic. When I heard them coming up the walk I went out and told them what had happened and sent them up to their rooms. At seven I drove over to the mayor's.

He had not come home but he was expected at any minute and I talked with his wife. She gave me a drink. By this time I was chain-smoking. When the mayor came in we went into a little office or library, where he took up a position behind a desk, putting me in the low chair of a supplicant. "Of course I sympathize with you, Moses," he said, "it's an awful thing to have happened, but the trouble is that we can't give you a zoning exception without a majority vote of the village council and all the members of the council happen to be out of town. Pete's in California and Jack's in Paris and Larry won't be back from Stowe until the end of the week."

I was sarcastic. "Then I suppose Cousin Justina will have to gracefully decompose in my parlor until Jack comes back from Paris."

"Oh no," he said, "oh *no*. Jack won't be back from Paris for another month but I think you might wait until Larry comes from Stowe. Then we'd have a majority, assuming of course that they would agree to your appeal."

"For Christ's sake," I snarled.

"Yes, yes," he said, "it is difficult, but after all you must realize that this is the world you live in and the importance of zoning can't be overestimated. Why, if a single member of the council could give out zoning exceptions, I could give you permission right now to open a saloon in your garage, put up neon lights, hire an orchestra and destroy the neighborhood and all the human and commercial values we've worked so hard to protect."

"I don't want to open a saloon in my garage," I howled. "I don't want to hire an orchestra. I just want to bury Justina."

"I know, Moses, I know," he said. "I understand that. But it's just that it happened in the wrong zone and if I make an exception for you I'll have to make an exception for everyone and this kind of morbidity, when it gets out of hand, can be very depressing. People don't like to live in a neighborhood where this sort of thing goes on all the time."

"Listen to me," I said. "You give me an exception and you give it to me now or I'm going home and dig a hole in my garden and bury Justina myself."

"But you can't do that, Moses. You can't bury anything in Zone B. You can't even bury a cat."

"You're mistaken," I said. "I can and I will. I can't function as a doctor and I can't function as an undertaker, but I can dig a hole in the ground and if you don't give me my exception, that's what I'm going to do."

"Come back, Moses, come back," he said. "Please

come back. Look, I'll give you an exception if you'll promise not to tell anyone. It's breaking the law, it's a forgery but I'll do it if you promise to keep it a secret."

I promised to keep it a secret, he gave me the documents and I used his telephone to make the arrangements. Justina was removed a few minutes after I got home but that night I had the strangest dream. I dreamed that I was in a crowded supermarket. It must have been night because the windows were dark. The ceiling was paved with fluorescent light—brilliant, cheerful but, considering our prehistoric memories, a harsh link in the chain of light that binds us to the past. Music was playing and there must have been at least a thousand shoppers pushing their wagons among the long corridors of comestibles and victuals. Now is there—or isn't there—something about the posture we assume when we push a wagon that unsexes us? Can it be done with gallantry? I bring this up because the multitude of shoppers seemed that evening, as they pushed their wagons, penitential and unsexed. There were all kinds, this being my beloved country. There were Italians, Finns, Jews, Negroes, Shropshiremen, Cubans—anyone who had heeded the voice of liberty—and they were dressed with that sumptuary abandon that European caricaturists record with such bitter disgust. Yes, there were grandmothers in shorts, big-butted women in knitted pants and men wearing such an assortment of clothing that it looked as if they had dressed hurriedly in a burning building. But this, as I say, is my own country and in my opinion the caricaturist who vilifies the old lady in shorts vilifies himself. I am a native and I was wearing buckskin jump boots, chino pants cut so tight that my sexual organs were discernible and a rayon-acetate pajama top printed with representations of the *Pinta,* the *Niña* and the *Santa María* in full sail. The scene was strange—the strangeness of a dream where we see familiar objects in an unfamiliar light—but as I looked more closely I saw that there were some irregularities. Nothing was labeled. Nothing was identified or known. The cans and boxes were all bare. The frozen-food bins were full of brown parcels but they were such odd shapes that you couldn't tell if they contained a frozen turkey or a Chinese dinner. All the goods at the vegetable and the bakery counters were concealed in brown bags and even the books for sale had no titles. In spite of the fact that the contents of nothing was known, my companions of the dream—my thousands of bizarrely dressed compatriots—were deliberating gravely over these mysterious containers as if the choices they made were critical. Like any dreamer, I was omniscient, I was with them and I was withdrawn, and stepping above the scene for a minute I noticed the men at the check-out counters. They were brutes. Now sometimes in a crowd, in a bar or a street, you will see a face so full-blown in its obdurate resistance to the appeals of love, reason and decency, so lewd, so brutish and unregenerate, that you turn away. Men like these were stationed at the only way out and as the shoppers approached them they tore their packages open—I still couldn't see what they contained—but in every case the customer, at the sight of what he had chosen, showed all the symptoms of the deepest guilt; that force that brings us to our knees. Once their choice had been opened to their shame they were pushed—in some cases kicked—toward the door and beyond the door I saw dark water and heard a terrible noise of moaning and crying in the air. They waited at the door in groups to be taken away in some conveyance that I couldn't see. As I watched, thousands and thousands pushed their wagons through the market, made their careful and mysterious choices and were reviled and taken away. What could be the meaning of this?

We buried Justina in the rain the next afternoon. The dead are not, God knows, a minority, but in Proxmire Manor their unexalted kingdom is on the outskirts, rather like a dump, where they are transported furtively as knaves and scoundrels and where they lie in an atmosphere of perfect neglect. Justina's life had been exemplary, but by ending it she seemed to have disgraced us all. The priest was a friend and a cheerful sight, but the undertaker and his helpers, hiding behind their limousines, were not; and aren't they at the root of most of our troubles, with their claim that death is a violet-flavored kiss? How can a people who do not mean to understand death hope to understand love, and who will sound the alarm?

I went from the cemetery back to my office. The commercial was on my desk and MacPherson had written across it in grease pencil: *Very funny, you broken-down bore. Do again.* I was tired but unrepentant and didn't seem able to force myself into a practical posture of usefulness and obedience. I did another commercial. *Don't lose your loved ones,* I wrote, *because of excessive radioactivity. Don't be a wallflower at the dance because of strontium 90 in your bones. Don't be a victim of fallout. When the tart on Thirty-sixth Street gives you the big eye does your body stride off in one direction and your imagination in another? Does your mind follow her up the stairs and taste her wares in revolting detail while your flesh goes off to Brooks Brothers or the foreign exchange desk of the Chase Manhattan Bank? Haven't you noticed the size of the ferns, the lushness of the grass, the bitterness of the string beans and the brilliant markings on the new breeds of butterflies? You have been inhaling lethal atomic waste for the last twenty-five years and only Elixircol can save you.* I gave this to Ralphie and waited perhaps ten minutes when it was returned, marked again with grease pencil. *Do, he wrote, or you'll be dead.* I felt very tired. I put another piece of paper into the machine and wrote: *The Lord is my shepherd; therefore can I lack nothing. He shall feed me in a green pasture and lead me forth beside the waters of comfort. He shall convert my soul and bring me forth in the paths of righteousness for his Name's sake. Yea, though I walk through the valley of the shadow of death I will fear no evil for thou art with me; thy rod and thy staff comfort me. Thou shalt prepare a table before me in the presence of them that trouble me; thou hast anointed my head with oil and my cup shall be full. Surely thy loving-kindness and mercy shall follow me all the days of my life and I will dwell in the house of the Lord for ever.* I gave this to Ralphie and went home.

BRIMMER

No one is interested in a character like Brimmer because the facts are indecent and obscene; but come then out of the museums, gardens, and ruins where obscene facts are as numerous as daisies in Nantucket. In the dense population of statuary around the Mediterranean shores there are more satyrs than there are gods and heroes. Their general undesirability in organized society only seems to have whetted their aggressiveness and they are everywhere; they are in Paestum and Syracuse and in the rainy courts and porches north of Florence.

They are even in the gardens of the American Embassy. I don't mean those pretty boys with long ears—although Brimmer may have been one of those in the beginning. I mean the older satyrs with lined faces and conspicuous tails. They always carry grapes or pipes, and the heads are up and back in attitudes of glee. Aside from the long ears, the faces are never animal—these are the faces of men, sometimes comely and youthful, but advanced age does not change in any way the lively cant of the head and the look of lewd glee.

I speak of a friend, an acquaintance anyhow—a shipboard acquaintance on a rough crossing from New York to Naples. These were his attitudes in the bar where I mostly saw him. His eyes had a pale, horizontal pupil like a goat's eye. Laughing eyes, you might have said, although they were sometimes very glassy. As for the pipes, he played, so far as I know, no musical instrument; but the grapes could be accounted for by the fact that he almost always had a glass in his hand. Many of the satyrs stand on one leg with the other crossed over in front—toe down, heel up—and that's the way he stood at the bar, his legs crossed, his head up in that look of permanent glee, and the grapes, so to speak, in his right hand. He was lively—witty and courteous and shrewd—but had he been much less I would have been forced to drink and talk with him anyhow. Excepting Mme

Troyan, there was no one else on board I would talk with.

How dull travel really is! How, at noon, when the whistle sounds and the band plays and the confetti has been thrown, we seem to have been deceived into join-ing something that subsists upon the patronage of the lonely and the lost—the emotionally second-rate of all kinds. The whistle blows again. The gangways and the lines are cleared and the ship begins to move. We see the faces of our dearly beloved friends and relations rubbed out by distance, and going over to the port deck to make a profoundly emotional farewell to the New York sky line we find the buildings hidden in rain. Then the chimes sound and we go below to eat a heavy lunch. Obsolescence might explain that chilling unease we ex-perience when we observe the elegance of the lounges and the wilderness of the sea. What will we do between now and tea? Between tea and dinner? Between dinner and the horse races? What will we do between here and landfall?

She was the oldest ship of the line and was making that April her last Atlantic crossing. Many seasoned travelers came down to say good-by to her famous in-teriors and to filch an ash tray or two, but they were sentimentalists to a man, and when the go-ashore was sounded they all went ashore, leaving the rest of us, so to speak, alone. It was a cheerless, rainy midday with a swell in the channel and, beyond the channel, gale winds and high seas. Her obsolescence you could see at once was more than a matter of marble fireplaces and grand pianos. She was a tub. It was not possible to sleep on the first night out, and going up on deck in the morning I saw that one of the lifeboats had been damaged in the gale. Below me, in second class, some undiscourageable travelers were trying to play Ping-pong in the rain. It was a bleak scene to look at and a hopeless prospect for the players and they finally gave up. A few minutes later a miscalculation of the helmsman sent a wall of water up the side of the ship and filled the stern deck with a boiling sea. Up swam the Ping-pong table and, as I watched, it glided overboard and could be seen bobbing astern in the wake, a reminder of how mysterious the world must seem to a man lost overboard.

Below, all the portable furniture had been corralled and roped together as if this place were for sale. Ropes were strung along all the passageways, and all the potted palm trees had been put into some kind of brig. It was hot—terribly hot and humid—and the elegant lounges, literally abandoned and very much abandoned in their atmosphere, seemed to be made, if possible, even more forlorn by the continuous music of the ship's orchestra. They began to play that morning and they played for the rest of the voyage and they played for no one. They played day and night to those empty rooms where the chairs were screwed to the floor. They played opera. They played old dance music. They played selections from *Show Boat*. Above the crashing of the mountainous seas there was always this wild, tiresome music in the air. And there was really nothing to do. You couldn't write letters, everything tipped so; and if you sat in a chair to read, it would withdraw itself from you and then rush up to press itself against you like some apple-tree swing. You couldn't play cards, you couldn't play chess, you couldn't even play Scrabble. The grayness, the thinly jubilant and continuous music, and the roped-up furniture all made it seem like an unhappy dream, and I wandered around like a dreamer until twelve-thirty when I went into the bar. The regulars in the bar then were a Southern family—Mother, Father, Sister, and Brother. They were going abroad for a year. Father had retired and this was their first trip. There were also a couple of women whom the bartender identified as a "Roman businesswoman" and her secretary. And there was Brimmer, myself, and presently Mme Troyan. I had drinks with Brimmer on the second day out. He was a man of about my age, I should say, slender, with well-kept hands that were, for some reason, noticeable, and a light but never monotonous voice and a charming sense of urgency—liveliness—that seemed to have nothing to do with nervousness. We had lunch and dinner together and drank in the bar after dinner. We knew the same places, but none of the same people, and yet he seemed to be an excellent companion. When we went below—he had the cabin next to mine—I was contented to have found someone I could talk with for the next ten days.

Brimmer was in the bar the next day at noon, and while we were there Mme Troyan looked in. Brimmer invited her to join us and she did. At my ripe age, Mme Troyan's age meant nothing. A younger man might have placed her in her middle thirties and might have noticed that the lines around her eyes were ineradicable. For me these lines meant only a proven capacity for wit and passion. She was a charming woman who did not mean to be described. Her dark hair, her pallor, her fine arms, her vivacity, her sadness when the bartender told us about his sick son in Genoa, her impersonations of the captain—the impression of a lovely and a brilliant woman who was accustomed to seeming delightful was not the listed sum of her charms.

We three had lunch and dinner together and danced in the ballroom after dinner—we were the only dancers —but when the music stopped and Brimmer and Mme Troyan started back to the bar I excused myself and went down to bed. I was pleased with the evening and when I closed my cabin door I thought how pleasant it would have been to have Mme Troyan's company. This was, of course, impossible, but the memory of her dark hair and her white arms was still strong and cheering when I turned out the light and got into bed. While I waited patiently for sleep it was revealed to me that Mme Troyan was in Brimmer's cabin.

I was indignant. She had told me that she had a husband and three children in Paris—and what, I thought, about them? She and Brimmer had only met by chance that morning, and what carnal anarchy would crack the world if all such chance meetings were consummated! If they had waited a day or two—long enough to give at least the appearance of founding their affair on some romantic or sentimental basis—I think I would have found it more acceptable. To act so quickly seemed to me skeptical and depraved. Listening to the noise of the ship's motors and the faint sounds of tenderness next door, I realized that I had left my way of life a thousand knots astern and that there is no inclination to internationalism in my disposition. They were both, in a sense, Europeans.

But the sounds next door served as a kind of trip wire: I seemed to stumble and fall on my face, skinning and bruising myself here and there and scattering my emotional and intellectual possessions. There was no point in pretending that I had not fallen, for when we are stretched out in the dirt we must pick ourselves up and brush off our clothes. This then, in a sense, is what I did, reviewing my considered opinions on marriage, constancy, man's nature and the importance of love. When I had picked up my possessions and repaired my appearance, I fell asleep.

It was dark and rainy in the morning—now the wind was cold—and I walked around the upper deck, four laps to the mile, and saw no one. The immorality next door would have changed my relationship to Brimmer and Mme Troyan, but I had no choice but to look forward to meeting them in the bar at noon. I had no resources to enliven a deserted ship and a stormy sea. My depraved acquaintances were in the bar when I went there at half-past twelve, and they had ordered a drink for me. I was content to be with them and thought perhaps they regretted what they had done. We lunched together, amiably, but when I suggested that we find a fourth and play some bridge Brimmer said that he had to send some cables and Mme Troyan wanted to rest. There was no one in the lounges or on the decks after lunch, and when the orchestra began, dismally, to tune up for their afternoon concert, I went down to my cabin where I discovered that Brimmer's cables and Mme Troyan's rest were both fabrications, meant, I suppose, to deceive me. She was in his cabin again. I went up and took a long walk around the deck with an Episcopalian clergyman. I found him to be a most interesting man, but he did not change the subject since he was taking a vacation from a parish where alcoholism and morbid promiscuity were commonplace. I later had a drink with the clergyman in the bar, but Brimmer and Mme Troyan didn't show up for dinner.

They came into the bar for cocktails before lunch on the next day. I thought they both looked tired. They must have had sandwiches in the bar or made some other arrangement because I didn't see them in the dining room. That evening the sky cleared briefly—it was the first clearing of the voyage—and I watched this from the stern deck with my friend, the minister. How much more light we see from an old ship than we see from the summit of a mountain! The cuts in the overcast, filled with colored light, the heights and reaches all reminded me of my dear wife and children and our farm in New Hampshire and the modest pyrotechnics of a sunset there. I found Mme Troyan and Brimmer in the bar when I went down before dinner, but they didn't know the sky had cleared.

They didn't see the Azores, nor were they around two

days later when we sighted Portugal. It was half-past four or five in the afternoon. First, there was some slacking off in the ship's roll. She was still rolling, but you could go from one place to another without ending up on your face, and the stewards had begun to take down the ropes and rearrange the furniture. Then on our port side we could see some cliffs and, above them, round hills rising to form a mountain, and on the summit some ruined fort or bastion—low-lying, but beautiful—and behind this a bank of cloud so dense that it was not until we approached the shore that you could distinguish which was cloud and which was mountain. A few gulls picked us up, and then villas could be seen, and there was the immemorial smell of inshore water like my grandfather's bathing shoes. Here was a different sea— catboats and villas and fish nets and sand castles flying flags and people calling in their children off the beach for supper. This was the landfall, and as I went up toward the bow I heard the Sanctus bell in the ballroom, where the priest was saying prayers of thanksgiving over water that has seen, I suppose, a million, million times the bells and candles of the Mass. Everyone was at the bow, as pleased as children to see Portugal. Everyone stayed late to watch the villas take shape, the lights go on, and to smell the shallows. Everyone but Brimmer and Mme Troyan, who were still in Brimmer's cabin

when I went down, and who couldn't have seen anything.

Mme Troyan left the ship at Gibraltar the next morning, when her husband was to meet her. We got there
at dawn—very cold for April—cold and bleak with snow
on the African mountains and the smell of snow in the
air. I didn't see Brimmer around, although he may have
been on another deck. I watched a deck hand put the
bags aboard the cutter, and then Mme Troyan walked
swiftly onto the cutter herself, wearing a coat over her
shoulders and carrying a scarf. She went to the stern
and began to wave her scarf to Brimmer or to me or to
the ship's musicians—since we were the only people she
had spoken to on the crossing. But the boat moved more
swiftly than my emotions and, in the few minutes it
took for my stray feelings of tenderness to accumulate,
the cutter had moved away from the ship, and the shape,
the color of her face was lost.

When we left Gibraltar, the potted palms were retired again, the lines were put up, and the ship's orchestra began to play. It remained rough and dreary.
Brimmer was in the bar at half-past twelve looking very
absent-minded, and I suppose he missed Mme Troyan. I
didn't see him again until after dinner, when he joined
me in the bar. Something, sorrow I suppose, was on his
mind, and when I began to talk about Nantucket (where

we had both spent some summers) his immense reservoirs of courtesy seemed taxed. He excused himself and left; half an hour later I saw that he was drinking in the lounge with the mysterious businesswoman and her secretary.

It was the bartender who had first identified this couple as a "Roman businesswoman" and her secretary. Then, when it appeared that she spoke a crude mixture of Spanish and Italian, the bartender decided that she was a Brazilian—although the purser told me that she was traveling on a Greek passport. The secretary was a hard-faced blonde, and the businesswoman was herself a figure of such astonishing unsavoriness—you might say evil—that no one spoke to her, not even the waiters. Her hair was dyed black, her eyes were made up to look like the eyes of a viper, her voice was guttural, and whatever her business was, it had stripped her of any appeal as a human being. These two were in the bar every night, drinking gin and speaking a jumble of languages. They were never with anyone else until Brimmer joined them that evening.

This new arrangement excited my deepest and my most natural disapproval. I was talking with the Southern family when, perhaps an hour later, the secretary strayed into the bar alone and ordered whiskey. She seemed so distraught that rather than entertain any obscene suspicions about Brimmer, I lit up the whole scene with an artificial optimism and talked intently with the Southerners about real estate. But when I went below I could tell that the businesswoman was in Brimmer's cabin. They made quite a lot of noise, and at one point they seemed to fall out of bed. There was a loud thump. I could have knocked on the door—like Carry Nation— ordering them to desist, but who would have seemed the most ridiculous?

But I could not sleep. It has been my experience, my observation, that the kind of personality that emerges from this sort of promiscuity embodies an especial degree of human failure. I say observation and experience because I would not want to accept the tenets of any other authority—any preconception that would diminish the feeling of life as a perilous moral adventure. It is difficult to be a man, I think; but the difficulties are not insuperable. Yet if we relax our vigilance for a moment we pay an exorbitant price. I have never seen such a relationship as that between Brimmer and the businesswoman that was not based on bitterness, irresolution and cowardice—the very opposites of love—and any such indulgence on my part would, I was sure, turn my hair white in a moment, destroy the pigmentation in my eyes, incline me to simper, and leave a hairy tail coiled in my pants. I knew no one who had hit on such a way of life except as an expression of inadequacy—a shocking and repugnant unwillingness to cope with the generous forces of life. Brimmer was my friend and consequently enough of a man to make him deeply ashamed of what he was doing. And with this as my consolation I went to sleep.

He was in the bar at twelve-thirty the next day, but I did not speak to him. I drank my gin with a German businessman who had boarded the ship at Lisbon. It may have been because my German friend was dull that I kept scrutinizing Brimmer for some telling fault—insipidity or bitterness in his voice. But even the full weight of my prejudice, which was immense, could not project, as I would have liked, traces of his human failure. He was just the same. The businesswoman and her secretary rejoined one another after dinner, and Brimmer joined the Southern family, who were either so obtuse or so naïve that they had seen nothing and had no objection to letting Brimmer dance with Sister and walk her around in the rain.

I did not speak to him for the rest of the voyage. We docked at Naples at seven o'clock on a rainy morning, and when I had cleared customs and was leaving the port with my bags, Brimmer called to me. He was with a good-looking, leggy blonde who must have been twenty years younger than he, and he asked if they could drive me up to Rome. Why I accepted, why I arose with such agility over my massive disapproval, seems to have been, in retrospect, a dislike of loneliness. I did not want to take the train alone to Rome. I accepted their offer and drove with them to Rome, stopping in Terracina for lunch. They were driving up to Florence in the morning, and since this was my destination, I went on with them.

Considering Brimmer's winning ways with animals and small children—they were all captivated—and his partiality (as I was to discover later) to the Franciscan forms of prayer, it might be worth recounting what happened that day when we turned off the road and drove up into Assisi for lunch. Portents mean nothing, but the truth is that when we begin a journey in Italy to a clap of thunder and a sky nearly black with swallows we pay more emotional attention to this spectacle than we would at home. The weather had been fair all that morning, but as we turned off toward Assisi a wind began to blow, and even before we reached the gates of the town the sky was dark. We had lunch at an inn near the duomo with a view of the valley and a good view of the storm as it came up the road and struck the holy city. It was darkness, wind and rain of an unusual suddenness and density. There was an awning over the window where we sat and a palm tree in a garden below us, and while we ate our lunch we saw both the awning and the palm tree picked to pieces by the wind. When we finished lunch it was like night in the streets. A young brother let us into the duomo, but it was too dark to see the Cimabues. Then the brother took us to the sacristy and unlocked the door. The moment Brimmer entered that holy place the windows exploded under the force of the wind, and it was only by some kind of luck that we were not all cut to pieces by the glass that flew against the chest where the relics are stored. For the moment or two that the door was opened, the wind ranged through the church, extinguishing every candle in the place, and it took Brimmer and me and the brother, all pulling, to get the door shut again. Then the brother hurried off for help, and we climbed to the upper church. As we drove out of Assisi the wind fell, and looking back I saw the clouds pass over the town and the place fill up and shine with the light of day.

We said good-by in Florence and I did not see Brimmer again. It was the leggy blonde who wrote to me in July or August, when I had returned to the United States and our farm in New Hampshire. She wrote from a hospital in Zurich, and the letter had been forwarded from my address in Florence. "Poor Brimmer is dying," she wrote. "And if you could get up here to see him I know it would make him very happy. He often speaks of you, and I know you were one of his best friends. I am enclosing some papers that might interest you since you are a writer. The doctors do not think he can live another week. . . ." To refer to me as a friend exposed what must have been the immensity of his loneliness; and it seemed all along that I had known he was going to die, that his promiscuity was a relationship not to life but to death. That was in the afternoon—it was four or five—the light glancing, and that gratifying stillness in the air that falls over the back country with the earliest signs of night. I didn't tell my wife. Why should I? She never knew Brimmer and why introduce death into such a tranquil scene? What I remember feeling was gladness. The letter was six weeks old. He would be dead.

I don't suppose she could have read the papers she sent on. They must have represented a time of life when he had suffered some kind of breakdown. The first was a facetious essay, attacking the modern toilet seat and claiming that the crouched position it enforced was disadvantageous to those muscles and organs that were called into use. This was followed by a passionate prayer for cleanliness of heart. The prayer seemed to have gone unanswered, because the next piece was a very dirty essay on sexual control, followed by a long ballad called

The Ups and Downs of Jeremy Funicular. This was a disgusting account of Jeremy's erotic adventures, describing many married and unmarried ladies and also one garage mechanic, one wrestler, and one lighthouse keeper. The ballad was long, and each stanza ended with a reprise lamenting the fact that Jeremy had never experienced remorse—excepting when he was mean to children, foolish with money, or overate of bread and meat at table. The last manuscript was the remains or fragments of a journal. *"Gratissimo Signore,"* he wrote, "for the creaking shutter, the love of Mrs. Pigott, the smells of rain, the candor of friends, the fish in the sea, and especially for the smell of bread and coffee, since they mean mornings and newness of life." It went on, pious and lewd, but I read no more.

My wife is lovely, lovely were my children and lovely that scene, and how dead he and his dirty words seemed in the summer light. I was glad of the news, and his death seemed to have removed the perplexity that he had represented. I could remember with some sadness that he had been able to convey a feeling that the exuberance and the pain of life was a glass against which his nose was pressed: that he seemed able to dramatize the sense of its urgency and its deadly seriousness. I remembered the fineness of his hands, the light voice, and the cast in his eye that made the pupil seem like a goat's;

but I wondered why he had failed, and by my lights he had failed horribly. Which one of us is not suspended by a thread above carnal anarchy, and what is that thread but the light of day? The difference between life and death seemed no more than the difference between going up to see the landfall at Lisbon and remaining in bed with Mme Troyan. I could remember the landfall —the pleasant, brackish smell of inshore water like my grandfather's bathing shoes—distant voices on a beach, villas, sea bells, and Sanctus bells, and the singing of the priest and the faces of the passengers all raised, all smiling in wonder at the sight of land as if nothing like it had ever been seen before.

But I was wrong, and set the discovery of my mistake in any place where you can find an old copy of *Europa* or *Epoca*. It is a Monday and I am spearfishing with my son off the rocks near Porto San Stefano. My son and I are not good friends, and it is at our best that we seem to be in disagreement with one another. We seem to want the same place in the sun. But we are great friends under water. I am delighted to see him there like a figure in a movie, head down, feet up, armed with a fishing spear, air streaming from his snorkel—and the rilled sand, where he stirs it, turning up like smoke. Here, in the deep water among the rocks, we seem to escape the tensions that make our relationships in other places vexatious. It is lovely here. With a little chop on the surface, the sun falls to the bottom of the sea in a great net of light. There are starfish in the colors of lipstick, and all the rocks are covered with white flowers. And after a *festa,* a Sunday when the beaches have been crowded, there are other things so many fathoms down—bits of sandwich paper, the crossword-puzzle page from *Il Messaggero,* and water-logged copies of *Epoca.* It is out of the back pages of one of these that Brimmer looks up to me from the bottom of the sea. He is not dead. He has just married an Italian movie actress. He has his left arm around her slender waist, his right foot crossed in front of his left and in his right hand the full glass. He looks no better and no worse, and I don't know if he has sold his lights and vitals to the devil or only discovered himself. I go up to the surface, shake the water out of my hair, and think that I am worlds away from home.

THE LOWBOY

Oh I hate small men and I will write about them no more but in passing I would like to say that's what my brother Richard is: small. He has small hands, small feet, a small waist, small children, a small wife, and when he comes to our cocktail parties he sits in a small chair. If you pick up a book of his, you will find his name, "Richard Norton," on the flyleaf in his very small handwriting. He emanates, in my opinion, a disgusting *aura* of smallness. He is also spoiled, and when you go to his house you eat *his* food from *his* china with *his* silver, and if you observe his capricious and vulgar house rules you may be lucky enough to get some of *his* brandy, just as thirty years ago one went into his room to play with *his* toys at *his* pleasure and to be rewarded with a glass of *his* ginger ale. Some people make less of an adventure than a performance of their passions. They do not seem to fall in love and make friends but to cast, with men, women, children, and dogs, some stirring drama that they were committed to producing at the moment of their birth. This is especially noticeable on the part of those whose casting is limited by a slender emotional budget. The clumsy performances draw our attention to the play. The ingénue is much too old. So is the leading lady. The dog is the wrong breed, the furniture is ill-matched, the costumes are threadbare, and when the coffee is poured there seems to be nothing in the pot. But the drama goes on with as much terror and pity as it does in more magnificent productions. Watching my brother, I feel that he has marshaled a second-rate cast and that he is performing, perhaps for eternity, the role of a spoiled child.

It is traditional in our family to display our greatest emotional powers over heirlooms—to appropriate sets of dishes before the will can be probated, to have tugs of war with carpets, and to rupture blood relationships over the subject of a rickety chair. Stories and tales that dwell on some wayward attachment to an object—a soup tureen or a lowboy—seem to narrow down to the texture of the object itself, the glaze on the china or the finish on the wood, and to generate those feelings of frustration that I, for one, experience when I hear harpsichord music. My last encounter with my brother involved a lowboy. Because our mother died unexpectedly and there was an ambiguous clause in her will, certain of the family heirlooms were seized by Cousin Mathilda. No one felt strong enough at the time to contest her claims. She is now in her nineties, and age seems to have cured her rapacity. She wrote to Richard and me saying that if she had anything we wanted she would be happy to let us have it. I wrote to say that I would like the lowboy. I remembered it as a graceful, bowlegged piece of furniture with heavy brasses and a highly polished veneer the color of cordovan. My request was halfhearted. I did not really care, but it seemed that my brother did. Cousin Mathilda wrote him that she was giving the lowboy to me, and he telephoned to say that he wanted it—that he wanted it so much more than I did that there was no point in even discussing it. He asked if he could visit me on Sunday—we live about fifty miles apart—and, of course, I invited him.

It was not his house or his whiskey that day, but it was his charm that he was dispensing and in which I was entitled to bask, and, noticing some roses in the garden that he had given my wife many years back, he said, "I see *my* roses are doing well." We drank in the garden. It was a spring day—one of those green-gold Sundays that excite our incredulity. Everything was blooming, opening, burgeoning. There was more than one could see—prismatic lights, prismatic smells, something that set one's teeth on edge with pleasure—but it was the shadow that was most mysterious and exciting, the light one could not define. We sat under a big maple, its leaves not yet fully formed but formed enough to hold the light, and it was astounding in its beauty, and seemed not like a single tree but one of a million, a link in a long chain of leafy trees beginning in childhood.

"What about the lowboy?" Richard asked.

"What about it? Cousin Mathilda wrote to ask if I wanted anything, and it was the only thing I wanted."

"You've never cared about those things."

"I wouldn't say that."

"But it's *my* lowboy!"

"Everything has always been yours, Richard."

"Don't quarrel," my wife said, and she was quite right. I had spoken foolishly.

"I'll be happy to buy the lowboy from you," Richard said.

"I don't want your money."

"What do you want?"

"I would like to know why you want the lowboy so much."

"It's hard to say, but I do want it, and I want it terribly!" He spoke with unusual candor and feeling. This seemed more than his well-known possessiveness. "I'm not sure why. I feel that it was the center of our house, the center of our life before Mother died. If I had one solid piece of furniture, one object I could point to, that would remind me of how happy we all were, of how we used to live . . ."

I understood him (who wouldn't?), but I suspected his motives. The lowboy was an elegant piece of furniture, and I wondered if he didn't want it for cachet, as a kind of family crest, something that would vouch for the richness of his past and authenticate his descent from the most aristocratic of the seventeenth-century settlers. I could see him standing proudly beside it with a drink in his hand. *My* lowboy. It would appear in the background of their Christmas card, for it was one of those pieces of cabinetwork that seem to have a countenance of the most exquisite breeding. It would be the final piece in the puzzle of respectability that he had made of his life. We had shared a checkered, troubled, and sometimes sorrowful past, and Richard had risen from this chaos into a dazzling and resplendent respectability, but perhaps this image of himself would be improved by the lowboy; perhaps the image would not be complete without it.

I said that he could have it, then, and his thanks were intense. I wrote to Mathilda, and Mathilda wrote to me. She would send me, as a consolation, Grandmother DeLancey's sewing box, with its interesting contents— the Chinese fan, the sea horse from Venice, and the invitation to Buckingham Palace. There was a problem of delivery. Nice Mr. Osborn was willing to take the lowboy as far as my house but no farther. He would deliver it on Thursday, and then I could take it on to Richard's in my station wagon whenever this was convenient. I called Richard and explained these arrangements to him, and he was, as he had been from the beginning, nervous and intense. Was my station wagon big enough? Was it in good condition? And where would I keep the lowboy between Thursday and Sunday? I mustn't leave it in the garage.

When I came home on Thursday the lowboy was there, and it was in the garage. Richard called in the middle of dinner to see if it had arrived, and spoke revealingly, from the depths of his peculiar feelings.

"Of course you'll let me have the lowboy?" he asked.

"I don't understand."

"You won't *keep* it?"

What was at the bottom of this, I wondered. Why should he endure jealousy as well as love for a stick of wood? I said that I would deliver it to him on Sunday, but he didn't trust me. He would drive up with Wilma, his small wife, on Sunday morning, and accompany me back.

On Saturday my oldest son helped me carry the thing from the garage into the hall, and I had a good look at it. Cousin Mathilda had cared for it tenderly and the ruddy veneer had a polish of great depth, but on the top was a dark ring—it gleamed through the polish like something seen under water—where, for as long as I could remember, an old silver pitcher had stood, filled with apple blossoms or peonies or roses or, as the summer ended, chrysanthemums and colored leaves. I remembered the contents of the drawers, gathered there like a precipitate of our lives: the dog leashes, the ribbons for the Christmas wreaths, golf balls and playing cards, the German angel, the paper knife with which Cousin Timothy had stabbed himself, the crystal inkwell, and the keys to many forgotten doors. It was a powerful souvenir.

Richard and Wilma came on Sunday, bringing a pile of soft blankets to protect the varnish from the crudities of my station wagon. Richard and the lowboy were united like true lovers, and, considering the possibilities of magnificence and pathos in love, it seemed tragic that he should have become infatuated with a chest of drawers. He must have had the same recollections as I when he saw the dark ring gleaming below the polish and looked into the ink-stained drawers. I have seen gardeners attached to their lawns, violinists to their instruments, gamblers to their good-luck pieces, and old ladies to their lace, and it was in this realm of emotion, as unsparing as love, that Richard found himself. He anxiously watched my son and me carry the thing out to the station wagon, wrapped in blankets. It was a little too big. The carved claw feet extended a few inches beyond the tail gate. Richard wrung his hands, but he had no alternative. When the lowboy was tucked in, we started off. He did not urge me to drive carefully, but I knew this was on his mind.

When the accident occurred, I could have been blamed in spirit but not in fact. I don't see how I could have avoided it. We were stopped at a toll station, where I was waiting for my change, when a convertible, full of adolescents, collided with the back of my car and splintered one of the bowed legs.

"Oh, you crazy fools!" Richard howled. "You crazy, thoughtless criminals!" He got out of the car, waving his hands and swearing. The damage did not look too great to me, but Richard was inconsolable. With tears in his eyes, he lectured the bewildered adolescents. The lowboy was of inestimable value. It was over two hundred years old. No amount of money, no amount of insurance could compensate for the damage. Something rare and beautiful had been lost to the world. While he raved, cars piled up behind us, horns began to blow, and the toll collector told us to move. "This is *serious,*" Richard said to him. When he had got the name and the registration of the criminal in the driver's seat, we went along, but he was terribly shaken. At his house we carried the injured antique tenderly into the dining room and put it on the floor in its wrappings. His shock seemed to have given way now to a glimmer of hope, and when he fingered the splintered leg you could see that he had begun to think of a future in which the leg would be repaired. He gave me a correct drink, and talked about his garden, as any well-mannered man in the face of a personal tragedy will carry on, but you could feel that his heart was with the victim in the next room.

Richard and I do not see much of one another, and we did not meet for a month or so, and when we did meet it was over dinner in the Boston airport, where we both chanced to be waiting for planes. It was summer —midsummer, I guess, because I was on the way to Nantucket. It was hot. It was getting dark. There was a special menu that night involving flaming swords. The cooked food—shish kebab or calves' liver or half a broiler —was brought to a side table and impaled on a small sword. Then a waiter would put what looked like cotton wool on the tip of the sword, ignite this, and serve the food in a blaze of fire and chivalry. I mention this not because it seemed comical or vulgar but because it was affecting to see, in the summer dusk, how delighted the good and modest people of Boston were with this show. While the flaming swords went to and fro, Richard talked about the lowboy.

What an adventure! What a story! First he had checked all the cabinetmakers in the neighborhood and found a man in Westport who could be relied upon to repair the leg, but when the cabinetmaker saw the lowboy he, too, fell in love. He wanted to buy it, and when Richard refused he wanted to know its history. When the thing was repaired, they had it photographed and sent the picture to an authority on eighteenth-century furniture. It was famous, it was notorious, it was the Barstow lowboy, made by the celebrated Sturbridge cabinetmaker in 1780 and thought to have been lost in a fire. It had belonged to the Pooles (our great-great-grandmother was a Poole) and appeared in their inventories until 1840, when their house was destroyed, but only the knowledge of its whereabouts had been lost. The piece itself had come down, safely enough, to us. And now it had been reclaimed, like a prodigal, by the most high-minded antiquarians. A curator at the Metropolitan had urged Richard to let the Museum have it on loan. A collector had offered him ten thousand dollars. He was enjoying the delicious experience of discovering that what he adored and possessed was adored by most of mankind.

I flinched when he mentioned the ten thousand dollars—after all, I could have kept the thing—but I did not want it, I had never really wanted it, and I sensed in the airport dining room that Richard was in some kind of danger. We said good-by then and flew off in different directions. He called me in the autumn about some business, and he mentioned the lowboy again. Did I remember the rug on which it had stood at home? I did. It was an old Turkey carpet, multicolored and scattered with arcane symbols. Well, he had found very nearly the same rug at a New York dealer's, and now the claw feet rested on the same geometric fields of brown and yellow. You could see that he was putting things together—he was completing the puzzle—and while he never told me what happened next, I could imagine it easily enough. He bought a silver pitcher and filled it with leaves and sat there alone one autumn evening drinking whiskey and admiring his creation.

It would have been raining on the night I imagined; no other sound transports Richard with such velocity backward in time. At last everything was perfect—the pitcher, the polish on the heavy brasses, the carpet. The chest of drawers would seem not to have been lifted into the present but to have moved the past with it into the room. Wasn't that what he had wanted? He would admire the dark ring in the varnish and the fragrance of the empty drawers, and under the influence of two liquids—rain and whiskey—the hands of those who had touched the lowboy, polished it, left their drinks on it, arranged the flowers in the pitcher and stuffed odds and ends of string into the drawers would seem to reach out of the dark. As he watched, their dull fingerprints clustered on the polish, as if this were their means of clinging to life. By recalling them, by going a step further, he evoked them, and they came down impetuously into the room—they flew—as if they had been waiting in pain and impatience all those years for his invitation.

First to come back from the dead was Grandmother DeLancey, all dressed in black and smelling of ginger. Handsome, intelligent, victorious, she had broken with the past, and the thrill of this had borne her along with the force of a wave through all the days of her life and, so far as one knew, had washed her up into the very gates of Heaven. Her education, she said scornfully, had consisted of learning how to hem a pocket handkerchief and speak a little French, but she had left a world where it was improper for a lady to hold an opinion and come into one where she could express her opinions on a platform, pound the lectern with her fist, walk alone in the dark, and cheer (as she always did) the firemen when the red wagon came helling up the street. Her manner was firm and oracular, for she had traveled as far west as Cleveland lecturing on women's rights. A lady could be anything! A doctor! A lawyer! An engineer! A lady could, like Aunt Louisa, smoke cigars.

Aunt Louisa was smoking a cigar as she flew in to join the gathering. The fringe of a Spanish shawl spread out behind her in the air, and her hoop earrings rocked as she made, as always, a forceful, a pressing entrance, touched the lowboy, and settled on the blue chair. She was an artist. She had studied in Rome. Crudeness, flamboyance, passion, and disaster attended her. She tackled all the big subjects—the Rape of the Sabines, and the Sack of Rome. Naked men and women thronged her huge canvases, but they were always out of drawing, the colors were dim, and even the clouds above her battlefields seemed despondent. Her failure was not revealed to her until it was too late. She poured her ambitions onto her oldest son, Timothy, who walked in sullenly from the grave, carrying a volume of the Beethoven sonatas, his face dark with rancor.

Timothy would be a great pianist. It was her decision. He was put through every suffering, deprivation, and humiliation known to a prodigy. It was a solitary and bitter life. He had his first recital when he was seven. He played with an orchestra when he was twelve. He went on tour the next year. He wore strange clothes, and used grease on his long curls, and killed himself when he was fifteen. His mother had pushed him pitilessly. And why should this passionate and dedicated woman have made such a mistake? She may have meant to heal or avenge a feeling that, through birth or misfortune, she had been kept out of the blessed company of contented men and women. She may have believed that fame would end all this—that if she were a famous painter or he a famous pianist, they would never again taste loneliness or know scorn.

Richard could not have kept Uncle Tom from joining them if he had wanted to. He was powerless. He had been too late in realizing that the fascination of the lowboy was the fascination of pain, and he had committed himself to it. Uncle Tom came in with the grace of an old athlete. He was the amorous one. No one had been able to keep track of his affairs. His girls changed weekly —they sometimes changed in midweek. There were tens, there were hundreds, there may have been thousands. He carried in his arms his youngest son, Peter, whose legs were in braces. Peter had been crippled just before his birth, when, during a quarrel between his parents, Uncle Tom pushed Aunt Louisa down the stairs.

Aunt Mildred came stiffly through the air, drew her

blue skirt down over her knees as she settled herself, and looked uneasily at Grandmother. The old lady had passed on to Mildred her emancipation, as if it were a nation secured by treaties and compacts, flags and anthems. Mildred knew that passivity, needlepoint, and housework were not for her. To decline into a contented housewife would have meant handing over to the tyrant those territories that her mother had won for eternity with the sword. She knew well enough what it was that she must not do, but she had never decided what it was that she should do. She wrote pageants. She wrote verse. She worked for six years on a play about Christopher Columbus. Her husband, Uncle Sidney, pushed the perambulator and sometimes the carpet sweeper. She watched him angrily at his housework. He had usurped her rights, her usefulness. She took a lover and, going for the first three or four times to the hotel where they met, she felt that she had found herself. This was not one of the opportunities that her mother had held out to her, but it was better than Christopher Columbus. Furtive love was the contribution she was meant to make. The affair was sordid and came to a sordid end, with disclosures, anonymous letters, and bitter tears. Her lover absconded, and Uncle Sidney began to drink.

Uncle Sidney staggered back from the grave and sat down on the sofa beside Richard, stinking of liquor. He had been drunk ever since he discovered his wife's folly. His face was swollen. His belly was so enlarged that it had burst a shirt button. His mind and his eyes were glazed. In his drunkenness he dropped a lighted cigarette onto the sofa, and the velvet began to smoke. Richard's position seemed confined to observation. He could not speak or move. Then Uncle Sidney noticed the fire and poured the contents of his whiskey glass onto the upholstery. The whiskey and the sofa burst into flame. Grandmother, who was sitting on the old pegged Windsor chair, sprang to her feet, but the pegs caught her clothing and tore the seat of her dress. The dogs began to bark, and Peter, the young cripple, began to sing in a thin voice—obscenely sarcastic—"Joy to the world! the Lord is come. Let Heaven and nature sing," for it was a Christmas dinner that Richard had reconstructed.

At some point—perhaps when he purchased the silver pitcher—Richard committed himself to the horrors of the past, and his life, like so much else in nature, took the form of an arc. There must have been some felicity, some clearness in his feeling for Wilma, but once the lowboy took a commanding position in his house, he seemed driven back upon his wretched childhood. We went there for dinner—it must have been Thanksgiving. The lowboy stood in the dining room, on its carpet of mysterious symbols, and the silver pitcher was full of chrysanthemums. Richard spoke to his wife and children in a tone of vexation that I had forgotten. He quarreled with everyone; he even quarreled with my children. Oh, why is it that life is for some an exquisite privilege and others must pay for their seats at the play with a ransom of cholers, infections, and nightmares? We got away as soon as we could.

When we got home, I took the green glass epergne that belonged to Aunt Mildred off the sideboard and smashed it with a hammer. Then I dumped Grandmother's sewing box into the ash can, burned a big hole in her lace tablecloth, and buried her pewter in the garden. Out they go—the Roman coins, the sea horse from Venice, and the Chinese fan. We can cherish nothing less than our random understanding of death and the earth-shaking love that draws us to one another. Down with the stuffed owl in the upstairs hall and the statue of Hermes on the newel post! Hock the ruby necklace, throw away the invitation to Buckingham Palace, jump up and down on the perfume atomizer from Murano and the Canton fish plates. Dismiss whatever molests us and challenges our purpose, sleeping or waking. Cleanliness and valor will be our watchwords. Nothing less will get us past the armed sentry and over the mountainous border.

THE DUCHESS

IF YOU SHOULD HAPPEN TO BE THE SON OF A COAL miner or were brought up (as I was) in a small town in Massachusetts, the company of a ranking duchess might excite some of those vulgar sentiments that have no place in fiction, but she was beautiful, after all, and beauty has nothing to do with rank. She was slender, but not thin. And rather tall. Her hair was ash blond, and her fine, clear brow belonged against that grandiose and shabby backdrop of limestone and marble, the Roman palace where she lived. It was hers, and, stepping from the shadows of her palace to walk along the river to early Mass, she never quite seemed to leave the grainy light. One would have been surprised but not alarmed to see her join the company of the stone saints and angels on the roof of Sant' Andrea della Valle. This was not the guidebook city but the Rome of today, whose charm is not the Colosseum in the moonlight, or the Spanish Stairs wet by a sudden shower, but the poignance of a great and an ancient city succumbing confusedly to change. We live in a world where the banks of even the most remote trout streams are beaten smooth by the boots of fishermen, and the music that drifts down from the medieval walls into the garden where we sit is an old recording of Vivienne Segal singing "Bewitched, Bothered and Bewildered"; and Donna Carla lived, like you and me, with one foot in the past.

She was Donna Carla Malvolio-Pommodori, Duchess of Vevaqua-Perdere-Giusti, etc. She would have been considered fair anywhere, but in Rome her blue eyes, her pale skin, and her shining hair were extraordinary. She spoke English, French, and Italian with equal style, but Italian was the only language she wrote correctly. She carried on her social correspondence in a kind of English: "Donna Carla thinks you for the flahers," "Donna Carla rekests the honor of your compagnie," etc. The first floor of her palace on the Tiber had been converted into shops, and she lived on the *piano nobile*. The two upper floors had been rented out as apartments. This still left her with something like forty rooms.

Most guidebooks carry the family history, in small print, and you can't travel in Italy without coming on those piles of masonry that Malvolio-Pommodoris have scattered everywhere, from Venice to Calabria. There were the three popes, the doge, and the thirty-six cardinals, as well as many avaricious, bloodthirsty, and dishonest nobles. Don Camillo married the Princess Plèves, and after she had given him three sons he had her excommunicated, on a rigged charge of adultery, and seized all her lands. Don Camillo and his sons were butchered at dinner by assassins who had been hired by their host, Don Camillo's uncle Marcantonio. Marcantonio was strangled by Cosimo's men, and Cosimo was poisoned by his nephew Antonio. The palace in Rome had had an oubliette—a dungeon below a chamber whose floor operated on the principle of a seesaw. If you walked or were pushed beyond the axis, you went howling down for good into the bone pit. All this was long before the nineteenth century, when the upper stories were remodeled into apartments. Donna Carla's grandparents were exemplary Roman nobles. They were even prudish, and had the erotic frescoes in the ballroom rectified. They were commemorated by a marble portrait statue in the smoking room. It was life-size and showed them as they might have appeared for a walk on the Lungo-Tevere—marble hats, marble gloves, a marble walking stick. He even had a marble fur collar on his marble . coat. The most corrupt and tasteless park commissioner could not have been bribed to give it space.

Donna Carla was born in the family village of Vevaqua, in Tuscany, where her parents lived for many years in a kind of exile. Her father was simple in his tastes, bold, pious, just, and the heir to an immense patrimony. Hunting in England as a young man, he had a bad spill. His arms and legs were broken, his skull was fractured, and several vertebrae were smashed. His parents took what was then the long trip from Rome to England, and waited three days for their brilliant son to regain consciousness. It was thought he would never walk again. His recuperative powers were exceptional, but it was two years before he took a step. Then, wasted, leaning on two sticks and half-supported by a busty nurse named Winifred-Mae Bolton, he crossed the threshold of the nursing home into the garden. He held his head up, smiled his quick smile, and moved haltingly, as if he were delayed by his pleasure in the garden and the air, and not by his infirmity. It was six months before he could return to Rome, and he returned with the news that he was going to marry Winifred-Mae Bolton. She had given him—literally—his life, and what, as a good

nobleman, could he do but give her his? The consterna-
tion in Rome, Milan, and Paris was indescribable. His
parents wept, but they were up against that single-
minded concern for probity that had appeared in his
character when he was a boy. His father, who loved him
as he loved his own life, said that Winifred-Mae would
not enter the gates of Rome so long as he lived, and she
did not.

Donna Carla's mother was a large cheerful woman
with a coronet of yellow-reddish hair and a very broad
manner. The only Italian she ever learned was *"prego"*
and *"grazie,"* and she pronounced these *"prygo"* and
"gryzia." During the years in exile in Vevaqua, she
worked in the garden. Her taste in formal gardening was
colored by the railroad-station gardens of England, and
she spelled out her husband's name—Cosimo—in pansies
and set it in a heart-shaped bed of artichokes. She liked
to fry fish and chips, for which the peasants thought she
was crazy. The only evidence that the Duke may have
regretted his marriage was an occasional—a charming—
look of bewilderment on his handsome face. With his
wife he was always loving, courteous, and protective.
Donna Carla was twelve years old when her grandparents died. After a period of mourning, she, Winifred-
Mae, and the Duke entered Rome by the gate of Santa
Maria del Popolo.

Winifred-Mae had probably, by then, seen enough of

ducal gigantism not to exclaim over the size of the palace on the Tiber. Their first night in Rome set the pattern for their life there. "Now that we're back in a city again," she said, "with all the shops and all, I'll go out and buy a bit of fresh fish, shall I, ducky, and fry it for you the way I used to when you were in hospital?" Perfect love was in the Duke's smile of assent. In the fish market she squealed at the squid and the eels, but she found a nice piece of sole, and took it home and fried it, with some potatoes, in the kitchen, while the servants watched with tears in their eyes to see the fall of such a great house. After dinner, as had been the custom in Vevaqua, she sang. It was not true that, as her enemies said, she had sung ditties and kicked up her petticoats in English music halls. She had sung in music halls before she became a nurse, but she had sung the "Méditation" from "Thaïs," and "The Road to Mandalay." Her display of talentlessness was exhaustive; it was stupendous. She seemed to hold her lack of talent up to the light for examination, and to stretch its seams. She flatted, and she sharped, and she strummed noisily on the piano, but she did all this with such perfect candor and self-assurance that the performance was refreshing. The Duke beamed at these accomplishments of his wife, and did not seem in any way inclined to compare this entertainment with the days of his youth, when he had stood with his nursemaid on the ballroom balcony and seen a quadrille danced by one emperor, two kings, three queens, and a hundred and thirty-six grand dukes and grand duchesses. Winifred-Mae sang for an hour, and then they turned out the lights and went to bed. In those years, an owl had nested in the palace tower, and they could hear, above the drifting music of fountains, the belling of the owl. It reminded Winifred-Mae of England.

Rome had intended never to make any acknowledgment of Winifred-Mae's existence, but a lovely duchessina who was also a billionairess was too good a thing to pass up, and it seemed that Donna Carla would be the richest woman in Europe. If suitors were to be presented to her, Winifred-Mae had to be considered, and she was called on by the high nobility. She went on cooking, sewing, singing, and knitting; they got her on her own terms. She was a scandal. She asked noble callers into the kitchen while she popped a steak-and-kidney pie into the oven. She made cretonne slipcovers for the furniture in the *salottino*. She complained, in explicit detail, about the old-fashioned plumbing in the palace. She installed a radio. At her insistence, the Duke employed as his secretary a young Englishman named Cecil Smith. Smith was not even liked by the English. Coming down the Spanish Stairs in the morning sun, he could remind you of the industrial Midlands. He smelled of Stoke-on-Trent. He was a tall man with brown curly hair parted and combed across his forehead like a drapery. He wore dark, ill-fitting clothes that were sent to him from England, and as a result of a fear of drafts and a fear of immodesty, he gave one the impression that he was buried in clothing. He wore nightcaps, undervests, mufflers and rubbers, and the cuff of his long underwear could be seen when he reached out his cup for another spot of tea, which he took with Winifred-Mae. His manners were refined. He wore paper cuffs and an eyeshade in the Duke's office, and he fried sausages and potatoes on a gas ring in his flat.

But the sewing, the singing, the smell of fish and chips, and Cecil Smith had to be overlooked by the needy nobility. The thought of what Donna Carla's grace and her billions could do to lubricate the aristocracy would make your heart thump. Potential suitors began coming to the palace when she was thirteen or fourteen. She was pleasant to them all. She had even then the kind of inner gracefulness that was to make her so persuasive as a young woman. She was not a solemn girl, but hilarity seemed to lie outside her range, and some countess who had come to display her son remarked afterward that she was like the princess in the fairy tale—the princess who had never laughed. There must have been some truth in the observation, because it stuck; people repeated the remark, and what they meant was an atmosphere of sadness or captivity that one sensed in spite of her clear features and her light coloring.

This was in the thirties—a decade, in Italy, of marching in the streets, arrests, assassinations, and the loss of familiar lights. Cecil Smith returned to England when the war broke out. Very few suitors came to the palace in those days. The crippled Duke was an implacable anti-Fascist, and he told everyone that Il Duce was an abomination and an infection, but he was never molested or thrown into prison, as were some less outspoken men; this may have been because of his rank, his infirmities, or his popularity with the Romans. But when the war began, the family was forced into a complete retirement. They were thought, wrongly, to be in sympathy with the Allies, and were allowed to leave the palace only once a day, to go to late or early Mass at San Giovanni. They were in bed and asleep on the night of September 10, 1943. The owl was hooting. Luigi, the old butler, woke them and said there was a messenger in the hall. They dressed quickly and went down. The messenger was disguised as a farmer, but the Duke recognized the son of an old friend. He informed the

Duke that the Germans were coming down the Via Cassia and were entering the city. The commanding general had put a price of a million lire on the Duke's head; it was the price of his intransigence. They were to go at once, on foot, to an address on the Janiculum. Winifred-Mae could hear the owl hooting in the tower, and she had never been so homesick for England. "I don't want to go, ducky," she said. "If they're going to kill us, let them kill us in our own beds." The Duke smiled kindly and opened the door for her onto one of the most troubled of Roman nights.

There were already German patrols in the streets. It was a long walk up the river, and they were very conspicuous—the weeping Englishwoman, the Duke with his stick, and the graceful daughter. How mysterious life must have seemed at that moment! The Duke moved slowly and had to stop now and then to rest, but though. he was in pain, he did not show it. With his head up and a price on it, he looked around alertly, as if he had stopped to observe or admire some change in his old city. They crossed the river by separate bridges and met at a barbershop, where they were taken into a cellar and disguised. Their skin was stained and their hair was dyed. They left Rome before dawn, concealed in a load of furniture, and that evening reached a small village in the mountains, where they were hidden in a farmhouse cellar.

The village was shelled twice, but only a few buildings and barns on the outskirts were destroyed. The farmhouse was searched a dozen times, by Germans and Fascists, but the Duke was always warned long in advance. In the village, they were known as Signor and Signora Giusti, and it was Winifred-Mae who chafed at this incognito. She was the Duchess Malvolio-Pommodori, and she wanted it known. Donna Carla liked being Carla Giusti. She went one day, as Carla Giusti, to the washing trough and spent a pleasant morning cleaning her clothes and gossiping with the other women. When she got back to the farm, Winifred-Mae was furious. She was Donna Carla; she must not forget it. A few days later, Winifred-Mae saw Donna Carla being taught by a woman at the fountain how to carry a copper vase on her head, and she called her daughter into the house and gave her another fierce lecture on rank. Donna Carla was always malleable and obedient, but without losing her freshness, and she never tried to carry a *conca* again.

When Rome was liberated, the family returned to the city, to find that the Germans had sacked the palace, and they then retired to an estate in the south and waited there for the war to end. The Duke was invited to help in the formation of a government, but he declined this invitation, claiming to be too old; the fact was that he supported, if not the King, the concept of monarchy.

The paintings and the rest of the family treasure were found in a salt mine and returned to the palace. Cecil Smith came back, put on his paper cuffs, and resumed the administration of the family fortune, which had come through the war intact. Suitors began to call on Donna Carla.

In the second year after the war, a hundred and seventeen suitors came to the palace. These were straight and honest men, crooked men, men suffering from hemophilia, and many cousins. It was Donna Carla's prerogative to propose marriage, and she saw them all to the door without hinting at the subject. This was a class of men whose disinheritedness was grandiose. Lying in bed in the Excelsior Hotel, they dreamed of what her wealth could do. The castle roof was repaired. Plumbing was installed at last. The garden bloomed. The saddle horses were fat and sleek. When she saw them to the door without having mentioned the subject of marriage, she offended them and she offended their dreams. She sent them back to a leaky castle and a ruined garden; she turned them out into the stormy weather of impoverished rank. Many of them were angry, but they kept on coming. She turned away so many suitors that she was finally summoned to the Vatican, where the Holy Father refreshed her sense of responsibility toward her family and its ancient name.

Considering that Winifred-Mae had upset the aristocratic applecart, she took a surprisingly fervid interest in the lineage of Donna Carla's suitors, and championed her favorites as they came. There was some hard feeling between the mother and daughter on this score, and—from Winifred-Mae—some hard words. More and more suitors came, and the more persistent and needy returned, but the subject of marriage was still not mentioned. Donna Carla's father confessor then suggested that she see a psychiatrist, and she was willing. She was never unwilling. He made an appointment for her with a devout and elderly doctor who practiced within the Catholic faith. He had been a friend of Croce's, and a large cabinet photograph of the philosopher hung on one of the dark walls of his office, but this may have been wasted on Donna Carla. He offered the Duchess a chair, and then, after some questioning, invited her to lie down on his couch. This was a massive piece of furniture, covered with worn leather and dating back to the earliest days of Freud. She walked gracefully toward the couch, and then turned and said, "But it is not possible for me to lie down in the presence of a gentleman." The doctor could see her point; it was a true impasse. She seemed to look longingly at the couch, but she could not change the facts of her upbringing, and so they said good-by.

The Duke was growing old. It was getting more and more difficult for him to walk, but this pain did not change his handsomeness and seemed only to increase his vitality. When people saw him, they thought, How nice it will be to eat a cutlet, take a swim, or climb a mountain; how pleasant, after all, life is. He passed on to Donna Carla his probity, and his ideal of a simple and elegant life. He ate plain fare off fine dishes, wore fine clothes in third-class train carriages, and, on the trip to Vevaqua, ate his simple lunch out of a basket. He kept —at great expense—his paintings cleaned and in good condition, but the dust covers on the chairs and chandeliers in the reception rooms had not been removed for years. Donna Carla began to interest herself in what she would inherit, and spent some time going over the ledgers in Cecil Smith's office. The impropriety of a beautiful Roman noblewoman's studying ledgers at a desk caused some gossip, and may have been the turning point in her reputation.

There was a turning point. Her life was not especially solitary, but her shy gracefulness gave this impression, and she had made enemies of enough of her former suitors to be the butt of gossip. It was said that the Duke's probity was miserliness and that the family's simple tastes were lunatic. It was said that the family ate bread crusts and canned sardines, and had only one electric-light bulb in the whole palace. It was said that they had gone crazy—all three of them—and would leave their billions to the dogs. Someone else said Donna Carla had been arrested for shoplifting on the Via Nazionale. Someone had seen her pick up a ten-lira piece on the Corso and put it in her bag. When Luigi, the old butler, collapsed on the street one day and was taken to the hospital in an ambulance, someone said that the doctors at the Clinic had found him dying of starvation.

The Communist party got on the band wagon and began to attack Donna Carla as the archetype of dying feudalism. A Communist deputy in the Chamber made a speech, saying that the sufferings of Italy would not be over until the Duchessina was dead. The village of Vevaqua voted Communist in the local elections. She went there after the harvest to audit the accounts. Her father was too frail and Smith was busy. She traveled third class, as she had been taught. The old calash and the shabby coachman were waiting for her at the station. Clouds of dust came from the leather cushions when she sat down. As the carriage was entering an olive grove below the walls of the village, someone threw a rock. It struck Donna Carla on the shoulder. Another stone struck her on the thigh and another on the breast. The coachman's hat was knocked off, and he whipped the horse, but the horse was too used to pulling a plow to change his pace. Then a stone hit the coachman on the forehead and blood spurted out. Blinded with blood, he dropped the reins. The horse moved over to the side of the road and began to eat grass. Donna Carla got out of the calash. The men in the olive grove ran off. She bound up the coachman's head with a scarf, took up the reins, and drove the old carriage up into the village, where "DEATH TO DONNA CARLA! DEATH TO THE DUCHESS!" was written everywhere. The streets were deserted. The servants in the castle were loyal, and they dressed her cuts and bruises, and they brought her tea, and cried. When she began the audit in the morning, the tenants came in, one by one, and she did not mention the incident. With grace and patience she went over the accounts with men she recognized as her assailants. Three days later she drove back through the olive grove and took the train, third class, to Rome.

But her reputation in Rome was not improved by this incident. Someone said that she had turned a starving child away from her door, that her avarice was pathological. She was smuggling her paintings into England and amassing a fortune there. She was selling the jewels. Noble Roman property owners are expected to be sharp, but stories of unusual dishonesty were fabricated and circulated about Donna Carla. It was also said that she was losing her looks. She was growing old. People disputed about her age. She was twenty-eight. She was thirty-two. She was thirty-six. She was thirty-eight. And she was still a familiar figure on the Lungo-Tevere, as grave and lovely as ever, with her shining hair and her half-smile. But what was the truth? What would a German prince, a suitor with a leaky palace, find if he went there for tea?

Prince Bernstrasser-Falconberg went under the massive arch at five one Sunday afternoon, into a garden where there were some tangerine trees and a fountain. He was a man of forty-five, with three illegitimate children, and with a jolly mistress waiting for him at the Grand Hotel. Looking up at the walls of the palace, he could not help thinking of all the good Donna Carla's wealth would do. He would pay his debts. He would buy a bathtub for his old mother. He would fix the roof. An old porter in yellow livery let him in, and Luigi opened a second pair of double doors, into a hall with a marble staircase. Donna Carla was waiting here in the dusk. "Awfully nice of you to come," she said, in English. "Frightfully gloomy, isn't it?" The fragile English music of her voice echoed lightly off the stones. The hall *was* gloomy, he could see, but this was only half the truth, and the Prince sensed at once that he was not supposed to notice that it was also stupendous. The young woman seemed to be appealing to him for some understanding of her embarrassment, of her dilemma at having to greet him in such surroundings, and of her wish to pretend that this was some quite ordinary hall, where two friends might meet on a Sunday afternoon. She gave him her hand, and apologized for her parents' absence, saying that they were unwell. (This was not quite the truth; Winifred-Mae had a cold, but the old Duke had gone off to a double feature.)

The Prince was pleased to see that she was attractive, that she had on a velvet dress and some perfume. He wondered about her age, and saw that her face, that close, seemed quite pale and drawn.

"We have quite a walk ahead of us," she said. "Shall we begin? The *salottino,* the only room where one can sit down, is at the other end of the palace, but one can't use the back door, because then one makes a *brutta figura. . . .*" They stepped from the hall into the cavernous picture gallery. The room was dimly lighted, its hundreds of chairs covered with chamois. The Prince wondered if he should mention the paintings, and tried to take his cue from the Duchess. She seemed to be waiting, but was she waiting for him to join her or waiting for a display of his sensibilities? He took a chance and stopped in front of a Bronzino and praised it. "He looks rather better now that he's been cleaned," she said. The Prince moved from the Bronzino to a Tintoretto. "I say," she said, "shall we go on to someplace more comfortable?"

The next gallery was tapestries, and her one concession to these was to murmur, "Spanish. A frightful care. Moths and all that sort of thing." When the Prince stopped to admire the contents of a cabinet, she joined him and explained the objects, and he caught for the first time a note of ambivalence in her apparent wish to be taken for a simple woman who lived in a flat. "Carved lapis lazuli," she said. "The vase in the center is supposed to be the largest piece of lapis lazuli in the world." Then, as if she sensed and regretted this weakening of her position, she asked, as they stepped into the next room, "Did you ever see so much rubbish?"

Here were the cradles of popes, the crimson sedan chairs of cardinals, the bread-and-butter presents of emperors, kings, and grand dukes piled up to the ceiling, and the Prince was confused by her embarrassment. What tack should he take? Her behavior was not what one would expect of an heiress, but was it, after all, so queer, so unreasonable? What strange attitudes might one not be forced into, saddled with a mile or more of paintings, burdened with the bulky evidence of four consecutive centuries of wealth and power? She might, playing in these icy rooms as a girl, have discovered in herself a considerable disinclination to live in a monument. In any event, she would have had to make a choice, for if she took this treasure seriously, it would mean living moment by moment with the past, as the rest of us live with our appetites and thirsts, and who would want to do that?

Their destination was a dark parlor. The Prince watched her stoop down to the baseboard and plug in a feeble lamp.

"I keep all the lamps unplugged, because the servants sometimes forget, and electricity is frightfully expensive in Rome. *There* we are!" she exclaimed, straightening up and gesturing hospitably to a sofa from which the worn velvet hung in rags. Above this was a portrait by Titian of the first Malvolio-Pommodori pope. "I make my tea on a spirit lamp, because in the time it takes the man to bring tea from the kitchen the water gets quite cold. . . ."

They sat waiting for the kettle to boil. She handed him his tea and smiled, and he was touched, although he didn't know why. But there seemed about this charming woman, as there was about so much that he admired in Rome, the threat of obsolescence. Her pallor was a little faded. Her nose was a little sharp. Her grace, her accent were close to excessive. She was not yet the kind of woman who carries her left hand adrift in midair, the little finger extended, as vulgar people are supposed to hold a teacup; her airs and graces were not yet mistaken, and through them the Prince thought he felt the beating of a healthy and decent heart. But he felt, at the same time, that her days ended inexorably in the damps of a lonely bed, and that much more of this life would transform her into that kind of wasted virgin whose musical voice has upon men the force of complete sexual discouragement.

"My mother regrets that she was unable to come to Rome," the Prince said, "but she asked me to express to you her hope that you will someday visit us in our country."

"How nice," Donna Carla said. "And please thank your mother. I don't believe we've ever met, but I do recall your cousins Otto and Friedrich, when they were in school here, and please remember me to them when you return."

"You should visit my country, Donna Carla."

"Oh, I would adore to, but I can't leave Rome, as things stand now. There is so much to do. There are the twenty shops downstairs and the flats overhead. Drains are forever bursting, and the pigeons nest in the tiles. I have to go to Tuscany for the harvests. There's never a minute."

"We have much in common, Donna Carla."

"Yes?"

"Painting. I love painting. It is the love of my life."

"Is that so?"

"I would love to live as you do, in a great house where one finds—how can I say it?—the true luminousness of art."

"Would you really? I can't say that I like it much myself. Oh, I can see the virtues in a pretty picture of a vase of flowers, but there's nothing like that here. Everywhere I look I see bloody crucifixions, nakedness, and cruelty." She drew her shawl closer. "I really don't like it."

"You know why I am here, Donna Carla?"

"Quite."

"I come from a good family. I am not young, but I am strong. I . . ."

"Quite," she said. "Will you have some more tea."

"Thank you."

Her smile, when she passed him his cup, was an open appeal to keep the conversation general, and he thought of his old mother, the Princess, taking her bath in a pail. But there was some persuasiveness, some triumphant intelligence in her smile that also made him feel, with shame, the stupidity and rudeness of his quest. Why should she want to buy his mother a bathtub? Why

should she want to fix his roof? Why had he been told
everything about the Duchess but the fact that she was
sensible? He could see her point. Indeed, he could see
more. He saw how idle the gossip had been. This
"swindler," this "miser," this "shoplifter" was no more
than a pleasant woman who used her head. He knew the
kind of suitors who had preceded him—more often than
not with a mistress waiting at the hotel—and why
shouldn't they have excited her suspicions? He knew
the brilliant society she had neglected; he knew its grim
card parties, its elegant and malicious dinners, its tedium,
not relieved in any way by butlers in livery and torchlit
gardens. How sensible of her to have stayed home. She
was a sensible woman—much too sensible to be interested in him—and what lay at the heart of the mystery
was her brains. No one would have expected to find
blooming in ancient Rome this flower of common sense.

He talked with her for twenty minutes. Then she rang
for Luigi and asked him to show the Prince to the door.

It came with a crash, the old Duke's death. Reading
Joseph Conrad in the *salottino* one night, he got up to
get an ash tray and fell down dead. His cigarette burned
in the carpet long after his heart had stopped beating.
Luigi found him. Winifred-Mae was hysterical. A cardi-
nal with acolytes rushed to the palace, but it was too

late. The Duke was buried in the great Renaissance tomb, surrounded by ruined gardens, on the Appia Antica, and half the aristocracy of Europe went into mourning. Winifred-Mae was shattered. She planned to return to England, but, having packed her bags, she found she was too ill to travel. She drank gin for her indigestion. She railed at the servants, she railed at Donna Carla for not having married, and then, after three months of being a widow, she died.

Every day for thirty days after her mother's death, Donna Carla left the palace in the morning for early Mass and then went out to the family tomb. Sometimes she drove. Sometimes she took a bus. Her mourning veil was so heavy that her features could hardly be seen. She went rain or shine, said her prayers, and was seen wandering in the garden in a thunderstorm. It made one sad to see her on the Lungo-Tevere; there seemed to be such finality to her black clothes. It made everyone sad —the beggars and the women who sold chestnuts. She had loved her parents too well. Something had gone wrong. Now she would spend the rest of her life—how easy this was to imagine—between the palace and the tomb. But at the end of thirty days Donna Carla went to her father confessor and asked to see His Holiness. A few days later, she went to the Vatican. She did not go bowling through the Piazza San Pietro in a hired limousine, wiping off her lipstick with a piece of Kleenex. She parked her dusty little car near the fountains and went through the gates on foot. She kissed His Holiness's ring, curtsied gracefully to the floor, and said, "I wish to marry Cecil Smith."

Wood smoke, confetti, and the smell of snow and manure spun on the wind on the changeable day when they were married, in Vevaqua. She entered the church as Donna Carla Malvolio-Pommodori, Duchess of Vevaqua-Perdere-Giusti, etc., and came out Mrs. Cecil Smith. She was radiant. They returned to Rome, and she took an office adjoining his, and shared the administration of the estate and the work of distributing her income among convents, hospitals, and the poor. Their first son—Cecil Smith, Jr.—was born a year after their marriage, and a year later they had a daughter, Jocelyn. Donna Carla was cursed in every leaky castle in Europe, but surely shining choirs of angels in heaven will sing of Mrs. Cecil Smith.

THE SCARLET MOVING VAN

GOOD-BY TO THE MORTAL BOREDOM OF DISTRIBUTING
a skinny chicken to a family of seven and all the other
rites of the hill towns. I don't mean the real hill towns
—Assisi or Perugia or Saracinesco, perched on a three-
thousand-foot crag, with walls the dispiriting gray of
shirt cardboards and mustard lichen blooming on the
crooked roofs. The land, in fact, was flat, the houses
frame. This was in the eastern United States, and the
kind of place where most of us live. It was the unin-
corporated township of B———, with a population of

perhaps two hundred married couples, all of them with dogs and children, and many of them with servants; it resembled a hill town only in a manner of speaking, in that the ailing, the disheartened, and the poor could not ascend the steep moral path that formed its natural defense, and the moment any of the inhabitants became infected with unhappiness or discontent, they sensed the hopelessness of existing on such a high spiritual altitude, and went to live in the plain. Life was unprecedentedly comfortable and tranquil. B—— was exclusively for the felicitous. The housewives kissed their husbands tenderly in the morning and passionately at nightfall. In nearly every house there were love, graciousness, and high hopes. The schools were excellent, the roads were smooth, the drains and other services were ideal, and one spring evening at dusk an immense scarlet moving van with gold lettering on its sides came up the street and stopped in the front of the Marple house, which had been empty then for three months.

The gilt and scarlet of the van, bright even in the twilight, was an inspired attempt to disguise the true sorrowfulness of wandering. "We Carry Loads and Part Loads to All Far-Distant Places," said the gold letters on the sides, and this legend had the effect of a distant train whistle. Martha Folkestone, who lived next door, watched through a window as the portables of her new neighbors were carried across the porch. "That looks like real Chippendale," she said, "although it's hard to tell in this light. They have two children. They seem like nice people. Oh, I wish there was something I could bring them to make them feel at home. Do you think they'd like flowers? I suppose we could ask them for a drink. Do you think they'd like a drink? Would you want to go over and ask them if they'd like a drink?"

Later, when the furniture was all indoors and the van had gone, Charlie Folkestone crossed the lawn between the two houses and introduced himself to Peaches and Gee-Gee. This is what he saw. Peaches was peaches—blond and warm, with a low-cut dress and a luminous front. Gee-Gee had been a handsome man, and perhaps still was, although his yellow curls were thin. His face seemed both angelic and menacing. He had never (Charlie learned later) been a boxer, but his eyes were slightly squinted and his square, handsome forehead had the conformation of layers of scar tissue. You might have said that his look was thoughtful until you realized that he was not a thoughtful man. It was the earnest and contained look of those who are a little hard of hearing or a little stupid.

They would be delighted to have a drink. They would be right over. Peaches wanted to put on some lipstick and say good night to the children, and then they would be right over. They came right over, and what seemed to be an unusually pleasant evening began. The Folkestones had been worried about who their new neighbors would be, and to find a couple as sympathetic as Gee-Gee and Peaches made them very high-spirited. Like everyone else, they loved to express an opinion about their neighbors, and Gee-Gee and Peaches were, naturally, interested. It was the beginning of a friendship, and the Folkestones overlooked their usual concern with time and sobriety. It got late—it was past midnight—and Charlie did not notice how much whiskey was being poured or that Gee-Gee seemed to be getting drunk. Gee-Gee became very quiet—he dropped out of the conversation—and then he suddenly interrupted Martha in a flat, unpleasant drawl.

"God, but you're stuffy people," he said.

"Oh, no, Gee-Gee!" Peaches said. "Not on our first night!"

"You've had too much to drink, Gee-Gee," Charlie said.

"Like hell I have," said Gee-Gee. He bent over and began to unlace his shoes. "I haven't had half enough."

"Please, Gee-Gee, please," Peaches said.

"I have to teach them, honey," Gee-Gee said. "They've got to learn."

Then he stood up and, with the cunning and dexterity of a drunk, got out of most of his clothing before anyone could stop him.

"Get out of here," Charlie said.

"The pleasure's all mine, neighbor," said Gee-Gee. He kicked over a hammered-brass umbrella stand on his way out the door.

"Oh, I'm frightfully sorry!" Peaches said. "I feel terribly about this!"

"Don't worry, my dear," Martha said. "He's probably very tired, and we've all had too much to drink."

"Oh, no," Peaches said. "It always happens. Everywhere. We've moved eight times in the last eight years, and there's never been anyone to say good-by to us. Not a soul. Oh, he was a beautiful man when I first knew him! You never saw anyone so fine and strong and generous. They called him the Greek God at college. That's why he's called Gee-Gee. He was All-America twice, but he was never a money player—he always played straight out of his heart. Everybody loved him. Now it's all gone, but I tell myself that I once had the love of a good man. I don't think many women have known that kind of love. Oh, I wish he'd come back. I wish he'd be the way he was. The night before last, when we were packing up the dishes in the old house, he got drunk and I slapped him in the face, and I shouted at him, 'Come back! Come back! Come back to me, Gee-Gee!' But he didn' listen. He didn't hear me. He doesn't hear anyone any more—not even the voices of his children. I ask myself every day what I've done to be punished so cruelly."

"I'm sorry, my dear!" Martha said.

"You won't be around to say good-by when we go," Peaches said. "We'll last a year. You wait and see. Some people have tender farewell parties, but even the garbage man in the last place was glad to see us go." With a grace and resignation that transcended the ruined evening, she began to gather up the clothing that her husband had scattered on the rug. "Each time we move, I think that the change will be good for him," she said. "When we got here tonight, it all looked so pretty and quiet that I thought he might change. Well, you don't have to ask us again. You know what it's like."

A few days or perhaps a week later, Charlie saw Gee-Gee on the station platform in the morning and saw how completely personable his neighbor was when he was sober. B—— was not an easy place to conquer, but Gee-Gee seemed already to have won the affectionate respect of his neighbors. Charlie could see, as he watched him standing in the sun among the other commuters, that he would be asked to join everything. Gee-Gee greeted Charlie heartily, and there was no trace of the ugliness he had shown that night. Indeed, it was impossible to believe that this charming and handsome man had been so offensive. In the morning light, and surrounded by new friends, he seemed to challenge the memory. He seemed almost able to transfer the blame onto Charlie.

Arrangements for the social initiation of the new couple were unusually rapid and elaborate, and began with a dinner party at the Watermans'. Charlie was already at the party when Gee-Gee and Peaches came in, and they came in like royalty. Arm in arm, radiant and beautiful, they seemed, at the moment of their entrance, to make the evening. It was a large party, and Charlie hardly saw them until they went in to dinner. He sat close to Peaches, but Gee-Gee was at the other end of the table. They were halfway through dessert when Gee-Gee's flat and unpleasant drawl sounded, like a parade command, over the general conversation.

"What a God-damned bunch of stuffed shirts!" he said. "Let's put a little vitality into the conversation, shall we?" He sprang onto the center of the table and began to sing a dirty song and dance a jig. Women screamed. Dishes were upset and broken. Dresses were ruined. Peaches pled to her wayward husband. The effect of this outrageous performance was to empty the dining room of everyone but Gee-Gee and Charlie.

"Get down off there, Gee-Gee," Charlie said.

"I have to teach them," Gee-Gee said. "I've got to teach them."

"You're not teaching anybody anything but the fact that you're a rotten drunk."

"They've got to learn," Gee-Gee said. "I've got to teach them." He got down off the table, breaking a few more dishes, and wandered out into the kitchen, where he embraced the cook, and then went on out into the night.

One might have thought that this was warning enough to a worldly community, but unusual amounts of forgiveness were extended to Gee-Gee. One liked him, and there was always the chance that he might not misbehave. There was always his charming figure in the morning light to confound his enemies, but it began to seem more and more like a lure that would let him into houses where he could break the crockery. Forgiveness was not what he wanted, and if he seemed to have failed at offending the sensibilities of his hostess he would increase and complicate his outrageousness. No one had ever seen anything like it. He undressed at the Bilkers'. At the Levys' he drop-kicked a bowl of soft cheese onto the ceiling. He danced the Highland fling in his underpants, set fire to wastebaskets, and swung on the Townends' chandelier—that famous chandelier. Inside of six weeks, there was not a house in B—— where he was welcome.

The Folkestones still saw him, of course—saw him in

his garden in the evening and talked to him across the hedge. Charlie was greatly troubled at the spectacle of someone falling so swiftly from grace, and he would have liked to help. He and Martha talked with Peaches, but Peaches was without hope. She did not understand what had happened to her Adonis, and that was as far as her intelligence took her. Now and then some innocent stranger from the next town or perhaps some newcomer would be taken with Gee-Gee and ask him to dinner. The performance was always the same, the dishes were always broken. The Folkestones were neighbors—there was this ancient bond—and Charlie may have thought that he could save the man. When Gee-Gee and Peaches quarreled, sometimes she telephoned Charlie and asked his protection. He went there one summer evening after she had telephoned. The quarrel was over; Peaches was reading a comic book in the living room, and Gee-Gee was sitting at the dining-room table with a drink in his hand. Charlie stood over his friend.

"Gee-Gee."

"Yes."

"Will you go on the wagon?"

"No."

"Will you go on the wagon if I go on the wagon?"

"No."

"Will you go to a psychiatrist?"

"Why? I know myself. I only have to play it out."

"Will you go to a psychiatrist if I go with you?"

"No."

"Will you do anything to help yourself?"

"I have to teach them." Then he threw back his head and sobbed, "Oh, Jesus . . ."

Charlie turned away. It seemed, at that instant, that Gee-Gee had heard, from some wilderness of his own, the noise of a distant horn that prophesied the manner and the hour of his death. There seemed to be some tremendous validity to the drunken man. Folkestone felt an upheaval in his spirit. He felt he understood the drunken man's message; he had always sensed it. It was at the bottom of their friendship. Gee-Gee was an advocate for the lame, the diseased, the poor, for those who through no fault of their own live out their lives in misery and pain. To the happy and the wellborn and the rich he had this to say—that for all their affection, their comforts, and their privileges, they would not be spared the pangs of anger and lust and the agonies of death. He only meant for them to be prepared for the blow when the blow fell. But was it not possible to accept this truth without having him dance a jig in your living room? He spoke from some vision of the suffering in life, but was it necessary to suffer oneself in order to accept his message? It seemed so.

"Gee-Gee?" Charlie asked.

"Yes."

"*What* are you trying to teach them?"

"You'll never know. You're too God-damned stuffy."

They didn't even last a year. In November, someone made them a decent offer for the house and they sold it. The gold-and-scarlet moving van returned, and they crossed the state line, into the town of Y———, where they bought another house. The Folkestones were glad to see them go. A well-behaved young couple took their place, and everything was as it had been. They were seldom remembered. But through a string of friends Charlie learned, the following winter, that Gee-Gee had broken his hip playing football a day or two before Christmas. This fact, for some reason, remained with him, and one Sunday afternoon when he had nothing much better to do he got Gee-Gee's telephone number from Information and called his old neighbor to say that he was coming over for a drink. Gee-Gee roared with enthusiasm and gave Charlie directions for getting to the house.

It was a long drive, and halfway there Charlie wondered why he had undertaken it. Y——— was several cuts below B———. The house was in a development, and the builder had not stopped at mere ugliness; he had constructed a community that looked, with its rectilinear windows, like a penal colony. The streets were named after universities—Princeton Street, Yale Street, Rutgers Street and so forth. Only a few of the houses had been sold, and Gee-Gee's house was surrounded by empty dwellings. Charlie rang the bell and heard Gee-Gee shouting for him to come in. The house was a mess, and as he was taking his coat off, Gee-Gee came slowly down the hall half-riding in a child's wagon, which he propelled by pushing a crutch. His right hip and leg were encased in a massive cast.

"Where's Peaches?" Charlie asked.

"She's in Nassau. She and the children went to Nassau for Christmas."

"And left you alone?"

"I wanted them to go. I made them go. Nothing can be done for me. I get along all right on this wagon. When I'm hungry, I make a sandwich. I wanted them to go. I made them go. Peaches needed a vacation, and I like being alone. Come on into the living room and make me a drink. I can't get the ice trays out—that's about the only thing I can't do. I can shave and get into bed and so forth, but I can't get the ice trays out."

Charlie got some ice. He was glad to have something to do. The image of Gee-Gee in his wagon had shocked him, and he felt a terrifying stillness over the place. Out of the kitchen window he could see row upon row of ugly, empty houses. He felt as if some hideous melodrama were approaching its climax. But in the living room Gee-Gee was his most charming, and his smile and his voice gave the afternoon a momentary equilibrium. Charlie asked if Gee-Gee couldn't get a nurse to stay with him. Couldn't someone be found to stay with him? Couldn't he at least rent a wheelchair? Gee-Gee laughed away all these suggestions. He was contented. Peaches had written him from Nassau. They were having a marvelous time.

Charlie believed that Gee-Gee had made them go. It was this detail, above everything else, that gave the situation its horror. Peaches would have liked, naturally enough, to go to Nassau, but she never would have insisted. She was much too innocent to have any envious dreams of travel. Gee-Gee would have insisted that she go; he would have made the trip so tempting that she could not, in her innocence, resist it. Did he wish to be left alone, drunken and crippled, in an isolated house? Did he need to feel abused? It seemed so. The disorder of the house and the image of his wife and children running, running, running on some coral beach seemed like a successful contrivance—a kind of triumph.

Gee-Gee lit a cigarette and, forgetting about it, lit another, and fumbled so clumsily with the matches that

Charlie saw that he might easily burn to death. Hoisting himself from the wagon into a chair, he nearly fell, and, if he were alone and fell, he could easily die of hunger and thirst on his own rug. But there might be some drunken cunning in his clumsiness, his playing with fire. He smiled slyly when he saw the look on Charlie's face. "Don't worry about me," he said. "I'll be all right. I have my guardian angel."

"That's what everybody thinks," Charlie said.

"Oh, but I have."

Outside, it had begun to snow. The winter sky was overcast, and it would soon be dark. Charlie said that he had to go. "Sit down," Gee-Gee said. "Sit down and have another drink." Charlie's conscience held him there a few moments longer. How could he openly abandon a friend—a neighbor, at least—to the peril of death? But he had no choice; his family was waiting and he had to go. "Don't worry about me," Gee-Gee said when Charlie was putting on his coat. "I have my angel."

It was later than Charlie had realized. The snow was heavy now, and he had a two-hour drive, on winding back roads. There was a little rise going out of Y——, and the new snow was so slick that he had trouble making the hill. There were steeper hills ahead of him. Only one of his windshield wipers worked, and the snow quickly covered the glass and left him with one small aperture onto the world. The snow sped into the head-lights at a dizzying rate, and at one place where the road was narrow the car slid off onto the shoulder and he had to race the motor for ten minutes in order to get back onto the hard surface. It was a lonely stretch there—miles from any house—and he would have had a sloppy walk in his loafers. The car skidded and weaved up every hill, and it seemed that he reached the top by the thinnest margin of luck.

After driving for two hours, he was still far from home. The snow was so deep that guiding the car was like the trickiest kind of navigation. It took him three hours to get back, and he was tired when he drove into the darkness and peace of his own garage—tired and in-finitely grateful. Martha and the children had eaten their supper, and she wanted to go over to the Lissoms' and discuss some school-board business. He told her that the driving was bad, and since it was such a short dis-tance, she decided to walk. He lit a fire and made a drink, and the children sat at the table with him while he ate his supper. After supper on Sunday nights, the Folkestones played, or tried to play, trios. Charlie played the clarinet, his daughter played the piano, and his older son had a tenor recorder. The baby wandered around underfoot. This Sunday night they played simple ar-rangements of eighteenth-century music in the pleas-antest family atmosphere—complimenting themselves when they squeezed through a difficult passage, and extending into the music what was best in their relationship. They were playing a Vivaldi sonata when the telephone rang. Charlie knew immediately who it was.

"Charlie, Charlie," Gee-Gee said. "Jesus. I'm in hot water. Right after you left I fell out of the God-damned wagon. It took me two hours to get to the telephone. You've got to get over. There's nobody else. You're my only friend. You've got to get over here. Charlie? You hear me?"

It must have been the strangeness of the look on Charlie's face that made the baby scream. The little girl picked him up in her arms, and stared, as did the other boy, at their father. They seemed to know the whole picture, every detail of it, and they looked at him calmly, as if they were expecting him to make some decision that had nothing to do with the continuing of a pleasant evening in a snowbound house—but a decision that would have a profound effect on their knowledge of him and on their final happiness. Their looks were, he thought, clear and appealing, and whatever he did would be final.

"You hear me, Charlie? You hear me?" Gee-Gee asked. "It took me damned near two hours to crawl over to the telephone. You've got to help me. No one else will come."

Charlie hung up. Gee-Gee must have heard the sound

of his breathing and the baby crying, but Charlie had said nothing. He gave no explanation to the children, and they asked for none. They knew. His daughter went back to the piano, and when the telephone rang again and he did not answer it, no one questioned the ringing of the phone. They seemed happy and relieved when it stopped ringing, and they played Vivaldi until nine o'clock, when he sent them up to bed.

He made a drink to diminish the feeling that some emotional explosion had taken place, that some violence had shaken the air. He did not know what he had done or how to cope with his conscience. He would tell Martha about it when she came in, he thought. That would be a step toward comprehension. But when she returned he said nothing. He was afraid that if she brought her intelligence to the problem it would only confirm his guilt. "But why didn't you telephone me at the Lissoms'?" she might have asked. "I could have come home and you could have gone over." She was too compassionate a woman to accept passively, as he was doing, the thought of a friend, a neighbor, lying in agony. She went on upstairs. He poured some whiskey into his glass. If he had called the Lissoms', if she had returned to care for the children and left him free to help Gee-Gee, would he have been able to make the return trip in the heavy snow? He could have put on chains, but when were the chains? Were they in the car or in the cellar? He didn't know. He hadn't used them that year. But perhaps by now the roads would have been plowed. Perhaps the storm was over. This last, distressing possibility made him feel sick. Had the sky betrayed him? He switched on the outside light and went hesitantly, unwillingly, toward the window.

The clean snow gave off an ingratiating sparkle, and the beam of light shone into empty and peaceful air. The snow must have stopped a few minutes after he had entered the house. But how could he have known? How could he be expected to take into consideration the caprices of the weather? And what about that look the children had given him—so stern, so clear, so like a declaration that his place at that hour was with them, and not with the succoring of drunkards who had forfeited the chance to be taken seriously?

Then the image of Gee-Gee returned, crushing in its misery, and he remembered Peaches standing in the hallway at the Watermans' calling, "Come back! Come back!" She was calling back the youth that Charlie had never known, but it was easy to imagine what Gee-Gee must have been—fair, high-spirited, generous, and strong —and why had it all come to ruin? *Come back! Come back!* She seemed to call after the sweetness of a summer's day—roses in bloom and all the doors and windows open on the garden. It was all there in her voice; it was like the illusion of an abandoned house in the last rays of the sun. A large place, falling to pieces, haunted for children and a headache for the police and fire departments, but, seeing it with its windows blazing in the sunset, one thinks that they have all come back. Cook is in the kitchen rolling pastry. The smell of chicken rises up the back stairs. The front rooms are ready for the children and their many friends. A coal fire burns in the grate. Then as the light goes off the windows, the true ugliness of the place scowls into the dusk with redoubled force, as, when the notes of that long-ago summer left Peaches' voice, one saw the finality and confusion of despair in her innocent face. *Come back! Come back!* He poured himself some more whiskey, and as he raised the glass to his mouth he heard the wind change and saw—the outside light was still on—the snow begin to spin down again, with the vindictive swirl of a blizzard. The road was impassable; he could not have made the trip. The change in the weather had given him sweet absolution, and he watched the snow with a smile of love, but he stayed up until three in the morning with the bottle.

He was red-eyed and shaken the next morning, and ducked out of his office at eleven and drank two Martinis. He had two more before lunch and another at four and two on the train, and came reeling home for supper. The clinical details of heavy drinking are familiar to all of us; it is only the human picture that concerns us here, and Martha was finally driven to speak to him. She spoke most gently.

"You're drinking too much, darling," she said. "You've been drinking too much for three weeks."

"My drinking," he said, "is my own God-damned business. You mind your business and I'll mind mine."

It got worse and worse, and she had to do something. She finally went to their rector—a good-looking young bachelor who practiced both psychology and liturgy—for advice. He listened sympathetically. "I stopped at the rectory this afternoon," she said when she got home that night, "and I talked with Father Hemming. He wonders why you haven't been in church, and he wants to talk to you. He's such a good-looking man," she added, trying to make what she had just said sound less like a planned speech, "that I wonder why he's never married." Charlie—drunk, as usual—went to the telephone and called the rectory. "Look, Father," he said. "My wife tells me that you've been entertaining her in the afternoons. Well, I don't like it. You keep your hands off my wife. You hear me? That damned black suit you wear doesn't cut any ice with me. You keep your hands off my wife or I'll bust your pretty little nose."

In the end, he lost his job, and they had to move, and began their wanderings, like Gee-Gee and Peaches, in the scarlet-and-gold van.

And what happened to Gee-Gee—what ever became of him? That boozy guardian angel, her hair disheveled and the strings of her harp broken, still seemed to hover over where he lay. After telephoning Charlie that night, he telephoned the fire department. They were there in eight minutes flat, with bells ringing and sirens blowing. They got him into bed, made him a fresh drink, and one of the firemen, who had nothing better to do, stayed on until Peaches got back from Nassau. They had a fine time, eating all the steaks in the deep freeze and drinking a quart of bourbon every day. Gee-Gee could walk by the time Peaches and the children got back, and he took up that disorderly life for which he seemed so much better equipped than his neighbor, but they had to move at the end of the year, and, like the Folkestones, vanished from the hill towns.

THE GOLDEN AGE

OUR IDEAS OF CASTLES, FORMED IN CHILDHOOD, ARE inflexible, and why try to reform them? Why point out that in a real castle thistles grow in the courtyard, and the threshold of the ruined throne room is guarded by a nest of green adders? Here are the keep, the drawbridge, the battlements and towers that we took with our lead soldiers when we were down with the chicken pox. The first castle was English, and this one was built by the king of Spain during an occupation of Tuscany, but the sense of imaginative supremacy—the heightened mystery of nobility—is the same. Nothing is inconsequential here. It is thrilling to drink Martinis on the battlements, it is thrilling to bathe in the fountain, it is even thrilling to climb down the stairs into the village after supper and buy a box of matches. The drawbridge is down, the double doors are open, and early one morning we see a family crossing the moat, carrying the paraphernalia of a picnic.

They are Americans. Nothing they can do will quite conceal the touching ridiculousness, the clumsiness of the traveler. The father is a tall young man, a little stooped, with curly hair and fine white teeth. His wife is pretty, and they have two sons. Both boys are armed with plastic machine guns, which were recently mailed to them by their grandparents. It is Sunday, bells are ringing, and who ever brought the bells into Italy? Not the *vaca* in Florence but the harsh country bells that bing and bang over the olive groves and the cypress alleys in such an alien discord that they might have come in the carts of Attila the Hun. This urgent jangling sounds over the last of the antique fishing villages—really one of the last things of its kind. The stairs of the castle wind down into a place that is lovely and remote. There are no bus or train connections to this place, no *pensions* or hotels, no art schools, no tourists or souvenirs; there is not even a post card for sale. The natives wear picturesque costumes, sing at their work, and haul up Greek vases in their fishing nets. It is one of the last places in the world where you can hear shepherds' pipes, where beautiful girls with loose bodices go unphotographed as they carry baskets of fish on their heads, and where serenades are sung after dark. Down the stairs come the Americans into the village.

The women in black, on their way to church, nod and wish them good morning. *"Il poeta,"* they say, to each other. Good morning to the poet, the wife of the poet, and the poet's sons. Their courtesy seems to embarrass the stranger. "Why do they call you a poet?" his older son asks, but Father doesn't reply. In the piazza there is some evidence of the fact that the village is not quite perfect. What has been kept out by its rough roads has come in on the air. The village boys roosting around the fountain have their straw hats canted over their foreheads, and matchsticks in their teeth, and when they walk they swagger as if they had been born in a saddle, although there is not a saddle horse in the place. The blue-green beam of the television set in the café has begun to transform them from sailors into cowboys, from fishermen into gangsters, from shepherds into juvenile delinquents and masters of ceremonies, their bladders awash with Coca-Cola, and this seems very sad to the Americans. *E colpa mia,* thinks Seton, the so-called poet, as he leads his family through the piazza to the quays where their rowboat is moored.

The harbor is as round as a soup plate, the opening lies between two cliffs, and on the outermost, the sea-ward cliff, stands the castle, with its round towers, that the Setons have rented for the summer. Regarding the nearly perfect scene, Seton throws out his arms and exclaims, "Jesus, what a *spot!*" He raises an umbrella at the stern of the rowboat for his wife, and quarrels with the boys about where they will sit. "You sit where I tell you to sit, Tommy!" he shouts. "And I don't want to hear another word *out* of you." The boys grumble, and there is a burst of machine-gun fire. They put out to sea in a loud but not an angry uproar. The bells are silent now, and they can hear the wheezing of the old church organ, its lungs rotted with sea fog. The inshore water is tepid and extraordinarily dirty, but out past the mole the water is so clear, so finely colored that it seems like a lighter element, and when Seton glimpses the shadow of their hull, drawn over the sand and rocks ten fathoms down, it seems that they float on blue air.

There are thongs for oarlocks, and Seton rows by standing in the waist and putting his weight against the oars. He thinks that he is quite adroit at this—even picturesque—but he would never, even at a great distance, be taken for an Italian. Indeed, there is an air of criminality, of shame about the poor man. The illusion of levitation, the charming tranquillity of the day—crenelated towers against that blueness of sky that seems to be a piece of our consciousness—are not enough to expunge his sense of guilt but only to hold it in suspense. He is a fraud, an impostor, an aesthetic criminal, and, sensing his feelings, his wife says gently, "Don't worry, darling, no one will know, and if they do know, they won't care." He is worried because he is not a poet, and because this perfect day is, in a sense, his day of reckoning. He is not a poet at all, and only hoped to be better understood in Italy if he introduced himself as one. It is a harmless imposture—really an aspiration. He is in Italy only because he wants to lead a more illustrious life, to at least broaden his powers of reflection. He has even thought of writing a poem—something about good and evil.

There are many other boats on the water, rounding the cliff. All the idlers and beach boys are out, bumping gunwales, pinching their girls, and loudly singing phrases of *canzone*. They all salute *il poeta*. Around the cliff the shore is steep, terraced for vineyards, and packed with wild rosemary, and here the sea has beaten into the shore a chain of sandy coves. Seton heads for the largest of these, and his sons dive off the boat as he approaches the beach. He lands, and unloads the umbrella and the other gear.

Everyone speaks to them, everyone waves, and everyone in the village but the few churchgoers is on the beach. The Setons are the only strangers. The sand is a dark-golden color, and the sea shines like the curve of a rainbow—emerald, malachite, sapphire, and indigo. The striking absence of vulgarity and censoriousness in the scene moves Seton so that his chest seems to fill up with some fluid of appreciation. This is simplicity, he thinks, this is beauty, this is the raw grace of human nature! He swims in the fresh and buoyant water, and when he has finished swimming he stretches out in the sun. But now he seems restless, as if he were troubled once more about the fact that he is not a poet. And if he is not a poet, then what is he?

He is a television writer. Lying on the sand of the cove, below the castle, is the form of a television writer. His crime is that he is the author of an odious situation comedy called "The Best Family." When it was revealed to him that in dealing with mediocrity he was dealing not with flesh and blood but with whole principalities and kingdoms of wrongdoing, he threw up his job and fled to Italy. But now "The Best Family" has been leased by Italian television—it is called "La Famiglia Tosta" over here—and the asininities he has written will ascend to the towers of Siena, will be heard in the ancient streets of Florence, and will drift out of the lobby of the Gritti Palace onto the Grand Canal. This Sunday is his début, and his sons, who are proud of him, have spread the word in the village. *Poeta!*

His sons have begun to skirmish with their machine guns. It is a harrowing reminder of his past. The taint of television is on their innocent shoulders. While the children of the village sing, dance, and gather wild flowers, his own sons advance from rock to rock, pretending to kill. It is a mistake, and a trivial one, but it flusters him, although he cannot bring himself to call them to him and try to explain that their adroitness at imitating the cries and the postures of the dying may deepen an international misunderstanding. They are misunderstood, and he can see the women wagging their heads at the thought of a country so barbarous that even little children are given guns as playthings. *Mamma mia!* One has seen it all in the movies. One would not dare walk on the streets of New York because of gang warfare, and once you step out of New York you are in a wilderness, full of naked savages.

The battle ends, they go swimming again, and Seton, who has brought along some spearfishing gear, for an hour explores a rocky ledge that sinks off the tip of the cove. He dives, and swims through a school of transparent fish, and farther down, where the water is dark and cold, he sees a large octopus eye him wickedly, gather up its members, and slip into a cave paved with white flowers. There at the edge of the cave he sees a Greek vase, an amphora. He dives for it, feels the rough clay on his fingers, and goes up for air. He dives again and again, and finally brings the vase triumphantly into the light. It is a plump form with a narrow neck and two small handles. The neck is looped with a scarf of darker clay. It is broken nearly in two. Such vases, and vases much finer, are often found along that coast, and if they are of no value they stand on the shelves of the café, the bakery, and the barbershop, but the value of this one to Seton is inestimable—as if the fact that a television writer could reach into the Mediterranean and bring up a Greek vase were a hopeful cultural omen, proof of his own worthiness. He celebrates his find by drinking some wine, and then it is time to eat. He polishes off the bottle of wine with his lunch, and then, like everyone else on the beach, lies down in the shade and goes to sleep.

Just after Seton had waked and refreshed himself with a swim, he saw the strangers coming around the point in a boat—a Roman family, Seton guessed, who had come up to Tarlonia for the weekend. There were a father, a mother, and a son. Father fumbled clumsily with the oars. The pallor of all three of them, and their attitudes, set them apart from the people of the village.

It was as if they had approached the cove from another continent. As they came nearer, the woman could be heard asking her husband to bring the boat up on the beach.

The father's replies were short-tempered and very loud. His patience was exhausted. It was not easy to row a boat, he said. It was not as easy as it looked. It was not easy to land in strange coves where, if a wind came up, the boat could be dashed to pieces and he would have to buy the owner a new boat. Boats were expensive. This tirade seemed to embarrass the mother and tire the son. They were both dressed for bathing and the father was not, and, in his white shirt, he seemed to fit that much less into the halcyon scene. The purple sea and the graceful swimmers only deepened his exasperation, and, red-faced with worry and discomfort, he called out excited and needless warnings to the swimmers, fired questions at the people on the shore (How deep was the water? How safe was the cove?), and finally brought his boat in safely. During this loud performance, the boy smiled slyly at his mother and she smiled slyly back. They had put up with this for so many years! Would it never end? Fuming and grunting, the father dropped anchor in two feet of water, and the mother and the son slipped over the gunwales and swam away.

Seton watched the father, who took a copy of *Il*

Tempo out of his pocket and began to read, but the light was too bright. Then he felt anxiously in his pockets to see if the house keys and the car keys had taken wing and flown away. After this, he scraped a little bilge out of the boat with a can. Then he examined the worn oar thongs, looked at his watch, tested the anchor, looked at his watch again, and examined the sky, where there was a single cloud, for signs of a tempest. Finally, he sat down and lit a cigarette, and his worries, flying in from all points of the compass, could be seen to arrive on his brow. They had left the hot-water heater on in Rome! His apartment and all his valuables were perhaps at that very moment being destroyed by the explosion. The left front tire on the car was thin and had probably gone flat, if the car itself had not been stolen by the brigands that you found in these remote fishing villages. The cloud in the west was small, to be sure, but it was the kind of cloud that heralded bad weather, and they would be tossed mercilessly by the high waves on their way back around the point, and would reach the *pensione* (where they had already paid for dinner) after all the best cutlets had been eaten and the wine had been drunk. For all he knew, the president might have been assassinated in his absence, the lira devalued. The government might have fallen. He suddenly got to his feet and began to roar at his wife and son. It was time to go, it was time to go. Night was falling. A storm was coming. They would be late for dinner. They would get caught in the heavy traffic near Fregene. They would miss all the good television programs. . . .

His wife and his son turned and swam back toward the boat, but they took their time. It was not late, they knew. Night was not falling, and there was no sign of a storm. They would not miss dinner at the *pensione.* They knew from experience that they would reach the *pensione* long before the tables were set, but they had no choice. They climbed aboard while the father weighed anchor, shouted warnings to the swimmers, and asked advice from the shore. He finally got the boat into the bay, and started around the point.

They had just disappeared when one of the beach boys climbed to the highest rock and waved a red shirt, shouting, *"Pesce cane! Pesce cane!"* All the swimmers turned, howling with excitement and kicking up a heavy surf, and swam for the shore. Over the bar where they had been one could see the fin of a shark. The alarm had been given in time, and the shark seemed surly as he cruised through the malachite-colored water. The bathers lined the shore, pointing out the menace to one another, and a little child stood in the shallows shouting, *"Brutto! Brutto! Brutto!"* Then everyone cheered as down the path came Mario, the best swimmer in the village, carrying a long spear gun. Mario worked as a stone-mason, and for some reason—perhaps his industriousness —had never fitted into the scene. His legs were too long or too far apart, his shoulders were too round or too square, his hair was too thin, and that luxuriance of the flesh that had been dealt out so generously to the other bucks had bypassed poor Mario. His nakedness seemed piteous and touching, like a stranger surprised in some intimacy. He was cheered and complimented as he came through the crowd, but he could not even muster a nervous smile, and, setting his thin lips, he strode into the water and swam to the bar. But the shark had gone, and so had most of the sunlight. The disenchantment of a dark beach moved the bathers to gather their things and start for home. No one waited for Mario; no one seemed to care. He stood in the dark water with his spear, ready to take on his shoulders the safety and wel-fare of the community, but they turned their backs on him and sang as they climbed the cliff.

To hell with "La Famiglia Tosta," Seton thought. To hell with it. This was the loveliest hour of the whole day. All kinds of pleasure—food, drink, and love—lay ahead of him, and he seemed, by the gathering shadow, gently disengaged from his responsibility for television from the charge of making sense of his life. Now every thing lay in the dark and ample lap of night, and the discourse was suspended.

The stairs they took went past the ramparts they had rented, which were festooned with flowers, and it was on this stretch from here up to the drawbridge and the portal, that the triumph of the King, the architect, and the stonemasons was most imposing, for one was involved in the same breath with military impregnability, princeliness, and beauty. There was no point, no turning, no tower or battlement where these forces seemed separate. All the ramparts were finely corniced, and at every point where the enemy could have been expected to advance, the great, eight-ton crest of the Christian King of Spain proclaimed the blood, the faith, and the good taste of the defender. Over the main portal, the crest had fallen from its fine setting of sea gods with tridents and had crashed into the moat, but it had landed with its blazonings upward, and the quarterings, the cross, and the marble draperies could be seen in the water.

Then, on the wall, among the other legends, Seton saw the words *"Americani, go home, go home."* The writing was faint; it might have been there since the war, or its faintness might be accounted for by the fact that it had been done in haste. Neither his wife nor his children saw it, and he stood aside while they crossed the drawbridge into the courtyard, and then he went back to rub the words out with his fingers. Oh, who could have written it? He felt mystified and desolate. He had been invited to come to this strange country. The invitations had been clamorous. Travel agencies, shipping firms, airlines, even the Italian government itself had besought him to give up his comfortable way of life and travel abroad. He had accepted the invitations, he had committed himself to their hospitality, and now he was told, by this ancient wall, that he was not wanted.

He had never before felt unwanted. It had never been said. He had been wanted as a baby, wanted as a young man, wanted as a lover, a husband and father, wanted as a scriptwriter, a raconteur and companion. He had, if anything, been wanted excessively, and his only worry had been to spare himself, to spread his sought-after charms with prudence and discretion, so that they would do the most good. He had been wanted for golf, for tennis, for bridge, for charades, for cocktails, for boards of management—and yet this rude and ancient wall addressed him as if he were a pariah, a nameless beggar, an outcast. He was most deeply wounded.

Ice was stored in the castle dungeon, and Seton took his cocktail shaker there, filled it, made some Martinis, and carried them up to the battlements of the highest tower, where his wife joined him to watch the light ring its changes. Darkness was filling in the honeycombed cliffs of Tarlonia, and while the hills along the shore bore only the most farfetched resemblance to the breasts of women, they calmed Seton's feelings and stirred in him the same deep tenderness.

"I might go down to the café after dinner," his wife said, "just to see what sort of a job they did with the dubbing."

She did not understand the strength of his feelings about writing for television; she had never understood. He said nothing. He supposed that, seen at a distance, on his battlement, he might have been taken for what he was not—a poet, a seasoned traveler, a friend of Elsa Maxwell's, a prince or a duke—but this world lying all about him now did not really have the power to elevate and change him. It was only himself—the author of "The Best Family"—that he had carried at such inconvenience and expense across borders and over the sea. The flowery and massive setting had not changed the fact that he was sunburned, amorous, hungry, and stooped, and that the rock he sat on, set in its place by the great King of Spain, cut into his rump.

At dinner, Clementina, the cook, asked if she might go to the village and see "La Famiglia Tosta." The boys, of course, were going with their mother. After dinner, Seton went back to his tower. The fishing fleet had begun to go out past the mole, their torches lighted. The moon rose and blazed so brightly on the sea that the water seemed to turn, to spin in the light. From the village he could hear the *bel canto* of mothers calling their girls, and, from time to time, a squawk from the television set. It would all be over in twenty minutes, but the sense of wrongdoing *in absentia* made itself felt in his bones. Oh, how could one stop the advance of barbarism, vulgarity and censoriousness? When he saw the lights his family carried coming up the stairs, he went down to the moat to meet them. They were not alone. Who was with them? Who were these figures ascending? The doctor? The mayor? And a little girl carrying gladioli. It was a delegation—and a friendly one, he could tell by the lightness of their voices. They had come to praise him.

"It was so beautiful, so comical, so true to life!" the doctor said.

The little girl gave him the flowers, and the mayor embraced him lightly. "Oh, we thought, *Signore*," he said, "that you were merely a poet."

THE WRYSONS

The Wrysons wanted things in the suburb of Shady Hill to remain exactly as they were. Their dread of change—of irregularity of any sort—was acute, and when the Larkin estate was sold for an old people's rest home, the Wrysons went to the Village Council meeting and demanded to know what sort of old people these old people were going to be. The Wrysons' civic activities were confined to upzoning, but they were very active in this field, and if you were invited to their house for cocktails, the chances were that you would be asked to sign an upzoning petition before you got away. This was something more than a natural desire to preserve the character of the community. They seemed to sense that there was a stranger at the gates—unwashed, tirelessly scheming, foreign, the father of disorderly children who would ruin their rose garden and depreciate their real-estate investment, a man with a beard, a garlic breath, and a book. The Wrysons took no part in the intellectual life of the community. There was hardly a book in their house, and, in a place where even cooks were known to have Picasso reproductions hanging above their wash-stands, the Wrysons' taste in painting stopped at marine sunsets and bowls of flowers. Donald Wryson was a large man with thinning fair hair and the cheerful air of a bully, but he was a bully only in the defense of rectitude, class distinctions, and the orderly appearance of things. Irene Wryson was not a totally unattractive woman, but she was both shy and contentious—especially contentious on the subject of upzoning. They had one child, a little girl named Dolly, and they lived in a pleasant house on Alewives Lane, and they went in for gardening. This was another way of keeping up the appearance of things, and Donald Wryson was very critical of a neighbor who had ragged syringa bushes and a bare spot on her front lawn. They led a limited social life; they seemed to have no ambitions or needs in this direction, although at

The Wrysons

Christmas each year they sent out about six hundred cards. The preparation and addressing of these must have occupied their evenings for at least two weeks. Donald had a laugh like a jackass, and people who did not like him were careful not to sit in the same train coach with him. The Wrysons were stiff; they were inflexible. They seemed to experience not distaste but alarm when they found quack grass in their lawn or heard of a contemplated divorce among their neighbors. They were odd, of course. They were not as odd as poor, dizzy Flossie Dolmetch, who was caught forging drug prescriptions and was discovered to have been under the influence of morphine for three years. They were not as odd as Caruthers Mason, with his collection of two thousand lewd photographs, or as odd as Mrs. Temon, who, with those two lovely children in the next room— But why go on? They were odd.

Irene Wryson's oddness centered on a dream. She dreamed once or twice a month that someone—some enemy or hapless American pilot—had exploded a hydrogen bomb. In the light of day, her dream was inadmissible, for she could not relate it to her garden, her interest in upzoning, or her comfortable way of life. She could not bring herself to tell her husband at breakfast that she had dreamed about the hydrogen bomb. Faced with the pleasant table and its view of the garden—faced even with rain and snow—she could not find it in herself to explain what had troubled her sleep. The dream cost her much in energy and composure, and often left her deeply depressed. Its sequence of events varied, but it usually went like this.

The dream was set in Shady Hill—she dreamed that she woke in her own bed. Donald was always gone. She was at once aware of the fact that the bomb had exploded. Mattress stuffing and a trickle of brown water were coming through a big hole in the ceiling. The sky was gray—lightless—although there were in the west a few threads of red light, like those charming vapor trails we see in the air after the sun has set. She didn't know if these were vapor trails or some part of that force that would destroy the marrow in her bones. The gray air seemed final. The sky would never shine with light again. From her window she could see a river, and now, as she watched, boats began to come upstream. At first, there were only two or three. Then there were tens, and then there were hundreds. There were outboards, excursion boats, yachts, schooners with auxiliary motors; there were even rowboats. The number of boats grew until the water was covered with them, and the noise of motors rose to a loud din. The jockeying for position in this retreat up the river became aggressive and then savage. She saw men firing pistols at one another, and a rowboat, in which there was a family with little children, smashed and sunk by a cruiser. She cried, in her drèam, to see this inhumanity as the world was ending. She cried, and she went on watching, as if some truth was being revealed to her—as if she had always known this to be the human condition, as if she had always known the world to be dangerous and the comforts of her life in Shady Hill to be the merest palliative.

Then in her dream she turned away from the window and went through the bathroom that connected their room and Dolly's. Her daughter was sleeping sweetly, and she woke her. At this point, her emotions were at their strongest. The force and purity of the love that she felt toward this fragrant child was an agony. She dressed the little girl and put a snowsuit on her and led her into the bathroom. She opened the medicine cabinet, the one place in the house that the Wrysons, in their passion for neatness, had not put in order. It was crowded with leftover medicines from Dolly's trifling illnesses—cough syrups, calamine lotion for poison ivy, aspirin, and physics. And the mild perfume of these remnants and the tenderness she had felt for her daughter when she was ill—as if the door of the medicine cabinet had been a window opening onto some dazzling summer of the emotions—made her cry again. Among the bottles was one that said "Poison," and she reached for this and unscrewed the top, and shook into her left hand a pill for herself and one for the girl. She told the trusting child some gentle lie, and was about to put the pill between her lips when the ceiling of the bathroom collapsed and they stood knee-deep in plaster and dirty water. She groped around in the water for the poison, but it was lost, and the dream usually ended in this way. And how could she lean across the breakfast table and explain her pallor to her husky husband with this detailed vision of the end of the world? He would have laughed his jack-ass laugh.

Donald Wryson's oddness could be traced easily enough to his childhood. He had been raised in a small town in the Middle West that couldn't have had much to recommend it, and his father, an old-fashioned commercial traveler, with a hothouse rose in his buttonhole and buff-colored spats, had abandoned his wife and his son when the boy was young. Mrs. Wryson had few friends and no family. With her husband gone, she got a job as a clerk in an insurance office, and took up, with her son, a life of unmitigated melancholy and need. She never forgot the horror of her abandonment, and she leaned so heavily for support on her son that she seemed to threaten his animal spirits. Her life was a Calvary, as she often said, and the most she could do was to keep body and soul together.

The Wrysons

She had been young and fair and happy once, and the only way she had of evoking these lost times was by giving her son baking lessons. When the nights were long and cold and the wind·whistled around the four-family house where they lived, she would light a fire in the kitchen range and drop an apple peel onto the stove lid for the fragrance. Then Donald would put on an apron and scurry around, getting out the necessary bowls and pans, measuring out flour and sugar, separating eggs. He learned the contents of every cupboard. He knew where the spices and the sugar were kept, the nut meats and the citron, and when the work was done, he enjoyed washing the bowls and pans and putting them back where they belonged. Donald loved these hours himself, mostly because they seemed to dispel the oppression that stood unlifted over those years of his mother's life—and was there any reason why a lonely boy should rebel against the feeling of security that he found in the kitchen on a stormy night? She taught him how to make cookies and muffins and banana bread and, finally, a Lady Baltimore cake. It was sometimes after eleven o'clock when their work was done. "We do have a good time together, don't we, son?" Mrs. Wryson would ask. "We have a lovely time together, don't we, you and me. Oh, hear that wind howling! Think of the poor sailors at sea." Then she would embrace him, she would run her fingers through his light hair, and sometimes, although he was much too big, she would draw him onto her lap.

All of that was long ago. Mrs. Wryson was dead, and when Donald stood at the edge of her grave he had not felt any very great grief. She had been reconciled to dying years before she did die, and her conversation had been full of gallant references to the grave. Years later, when Donald was living alone in New York, he had been overtaken suddenly, one spring evening, by a depression as keen as any in his adolescence. He did not drink, he did not enjoy books or movies or the theatre, and, like his mother, he had few friends. Searching desperately for some way to take himself out of this misery, he hit on the idea of baking a Lady Baltimore cake. He went out and bought the ingredients—deeply ashamed of himself—and sifted the flour and chopped the nuts and citron in the kitchen of the little walk-up apartment where he lived. As he stirred the cake batter, he felt his depression vanish. It was not until he had put the cake in the oven and sat down to wipe his hands on his apron that he realized how successful he had been in summoning the ghost of his mother and the sense of security he had experienced as a child in her kitchen on stormy nights. When the cake was done he iced it, ate a slice and dumped the rest into the garbage.

The next time he felt troubled, he resisted the temp

tation to bake a cake, but he was not always able to do this, and during the eight or nine years he had been married to Irene he must have baked eight or nine cakes. He took extraordinary precautions, and she knew nothing of this. She believed him to be a complete stranger to the kitchen. And how could he at the breakfast table —all two hundred and sixteen pounds of him—explain that he looked sleepy because he had been up until three baking a Lady Baltimore cake, which he had hidden in the garage?

Given these unpleasant facts, then, about these not attractive people, we can dispatch them brightly enough, and who but Dolly would ever miss them? Donald Wryson, in his crusading zeal for upzoning, was out in all kinds of weather, and let's say that one night, when he was returning from a referendum in an ice storm, his car skidded down Hill Street, struck the big elm at the corner, and was demolished. Finis. His poor widow, either through love or dependence, was inconsolable. Getting out of bed one morning, a month or so after the loss of her husband, she got her feet caught in the dust ruffle and fell and broke her hip. Weakened by a long convalescence, she contracted pneumonia and departed this life. This leaves us with Dolly to account for, and what a sad tale we can write for this little girl. During the months in which her parents' will is in probate, she lives first on the charity and then on the forbearance of her neighbors. Finally, she is sent to live with her only relative, a cousin of her mother's, who is a schoolteacher in Los Angeles. How many hundreds of nights will she cry herself to sleep in bewilderment and loneliness. How strange and cold the world will seem. There is little to remind her of her parents except at Christmas, when, forwarded from Shady Hill, will come Greetings from Mrs. Sallust Trevor, who has been living in Paris and does not know about the accident; Salutations from the Parkers, who live in Mexico and never did get their lists straight; Season's Greetings from Meyers' Drugstore; Merry Christmas from the Perry Browns; Santissimas from the Oak Tree Italian Restaurant; A Joyeux Noël from Dodie Smith. Year after year, it will be this little girl's responsibility to throw into the wastebasket these cheerful holiday greetings that have followed her parents to and beyond the grave. . . . But this did not happen, and if it had, it would have thrown no light on what we know.

What happened was this. Irene Wryson had her dream one night. When she woke, she saw that her husband was not in bed. The air smelled sweet. Sweating suddenly, the beating of her heart strained with terror, she realized that the end had come. What could that sweetness in the air be but atomic ash? She ran to the window, but the river was empty. Half asleep and feeling cruelly lost as she was, she was kept from waking Dolly only by a healthy curiosity. There was smoke in the hallway, but it was not the smoke of any common fire. The sweetness made her feel sure that this was lethal ash. Led on by the smell, she went on down the stairs and through the dining room into the lighted kitchen. Donald was asleep with his head on the table and the room was full of smoke. "Oh, my darling," she cried, and woke him.

"I burned it," he said when he saw the smoke pouring from the oven. "I burned the damned thing."

"I thought it was the hydrogen bomb," she said.

"It's a cake," he said. "I burned it. What made you think it was the hydrogen bomb?"

"If you wanted something to eat, you should have waked me," she said.

She turned off the oven, and opened the window to let out the smell of smoke and let in the smell of nicotiana and other night flowers. She may have hesitated for a moment, for what would the stranger at the gates—that intruder with his beard and his book—have made of this couple, in their night clothes, in the smoke-filled kitchen at half past four in the morning? Some comprehension —perhaps momentary—of the complexity of life must have come to them, but it was only momentary. There were no further explanations. He threw the cake, which was burned to a cinder, into the garbage, and they turned out the lights and climbed the stairs, more mystified by life than ever, and more interested than ever in a good appearance.

BOY IN ROME

IT IS RAINING IN ROME (THE BOY WROTE) WHERE we live in a palace with a golden ceiling and where the wisteria is in bloom but you can't hear the noise of the rain in Rome. In the beginning we used to spend the summers in Nantucket and the winters in Rome and in Nantucket you can hear the rain and I like to lie in bed at night and listen to it running in the grass like fire because then you can see in what they call the mind's eye the number of different things that grow in the sea pastures there like heather and clover and fern. We used to come down to New York in the fall and sail in October and the best record of those trips would be the pictures the ship's photographer used to take and post in the library after the whoopee: I mean men wearing lady's hats and old people playing musical chairs and the whole thing lit by flash bulbs so that it looked like a thunderstorm in a forest. I used to play Ping-pong with the old people and I always won the Ping-pong tournament on the eastward crossing. I won a pigskin wallet on the Italian Line and a pen and pencil set on American Export and three handkerchiefs from the Home Lines, and once we traveled on a Greek ship where I won a cigarette lighter. I gave the cigarette lighter to my father because in those days I didn't drink, smoke, swear, or speak Italian.

My father was kind to me and when I was little he took me to the zoo, and let me ride horseback, and always bought me some pastry and an orangeade at a café, and while I drank my orangeade he always had a vermouth with a double shot of gin or later when there were so many Americans in Rome a Martini but I am not writing a story about a boy who sees his father sneaking drinks. The only time I spoke Italian then was when my father and I would visit the raven in the Borghese Gardens and feed him peanuts. When the raven saw us he would say *buon giorno* and I would say *buon giorno* and then when I gave him the peanuts he would say *grazie* and then when we walked away he would say *ciao*. My father died three years ago and he was buried in the Protestant Cemetery in Rome. There were a lot of people there and at the end of it my mother put an arm around me and she said, "We won't *ever* leave him alone here, will we, Pietro? We won't ever, *ever*, leave him alone here, will we, dear?" So some Americans live in Rome because of the income tax and some Americans live in Rome because they're divorced or oversexed or poetic or have some other reason for feeling that they might be persecuted at home and some Americans live in Rome because they work there, but we live in Rome because my father's bones lie in the Protestant Cemetery.

My grandfather was a tycoon and I think that is why my father liked to live in Rome. My grandfather started life with nothing at all, but he made plenty and he expected everybody else to do what he did, although this was not possible. The only time I ever saw much of my grandfather was when we used to visit him at his summer house in Colorado. The thing I remember mostly is the Sunday-night suppers which my grandfather used to cook when the maids and the cook were off. He always cooked a steak and even before he got the fire started everybody would be so nervous that you lost your appetite. He always had a terrible time getting the fire started and everyone sat around watching him, but you didn't dare say a word. There was no drinking because he didn't approve of drinking, but my parents used to drink plenty in the bathroom. Well, after it took him half an hour to get the fire started, he would put the steak on the grill and we would all go on sitting there. What made everyone nervous was that they knew they were going to be judged. If we had done anything wrong during the week that grampa disliked, well now we would know about it. He used to practically have a fit just cooking a steak. When the fat caught on fire his face would turn purple and he would jump up and down and run around. When the steak was done we would each get a dinner plate and stand in line and this was the judgment. If grampa liked you he would give you a nice piece of meat, but if he felt or suspected that you had done something wrong he would give you only a tiny piece of gristle. Well, you'd be surprised how embarrassing it is to find yourself holding this big plate with just a bit of gristle on it. You feel awful.

One week I tried to do everything right so I would not get a piece of gristle. I washed the station wagon and helped grandma in the garden and brought in wood for the house fires, but all I got on Sunday was a little bit of gristle. So then I said, *Grampa*, I said, *I don't under-*

stand why you cook steak for us every Sunday if it makes
you so unhappy. Mother knows how to cook and she
could at least scramble some eggs and I know how to
make sandwiches. I could make sandwiches. I mean if
you want to cook for us that would be nice but it looks
to me like you don't and I think it would be nicer if
instead of going through this torture chamber we just
had some scrambled eggs in the kitchen. I mean I don't
see why if you ask people to have supper with you it
should make you so irritable. Well, he put down his
knife and his fork and I've seen his face get purple
when the fat was burning, but I've never seen it get so
purple as it did that night. *You God-damned weak-
minded, parasitic ape,* he shouted at me, and then he
went into the house and upstairs to his bedroom, slam-
ming about every door he passed, and my mother took me
down into the garden and told me I had made an awful
mistake, but I couldn't see that I had done anything
wrong. But in a little while I could hear my father and
my grandfather yelling and swearing at one another and
in the morning we went away and we never came back
and when he died he left me one dollar.

It was the next year that my father died and I missed
him. It is against everything I believe in and not even
the kind of thing I am interested in, but I used to think
that he would come back from the kingdom of the dead

and give me help. I have the head and shoulders to do a man's work, but sometimes I am disappointed in my maturity and my disappointment in myself is deepest when I get off a train at the end of the day in a city that isn't my home like Florence with the *tramontana* blowing and no one in the square in front of the station who doesn't have to be there because of that merciless wind. Then it seems that I am not like myself or the sum of what I have learned but that I am stripped of my emotional savings by the *tramontana* and the hour and the strangeness of the place and I do not know which way to turn except of course to turn away from the wind. It was like that when I went alone on the train to Florence and the *tramontana* was blowing and there was no one in the piazza. I was feeling lonely and then some-one touched me on the shoulder and I thought it was my father come back from the kingdom of the dead and that we would all be happy together again and help one another. Who touched me was a ragged old man who was trying to sell me some souvenir key rings and when I saw the sores on his face I felt worse than ever and it seemed to me that there was a big hole torn in my life and that I was never going to get all the loving I needed and that autumn once in Rome I stayed late in school and was coming home on the trolley car and it was after seven and all the stores and offices were closing and

everybody was going home and rushed and someone
touched me on the shoulder and I thought it was my
father come again from the kingdom of the dead. I
didn't even look around this time because it could have
been anybody—a priest or a tart or an old man who had
lost his balance—but I had the same feeling that we
would all be happy together again and then I knew that
I was never going to get all the loving I needed, no,
never.

After my father passed away we gave up the trips to
Nantucket and lived all the time in the Palazzo Orvieta.
This is a beautiful and a somber building with a famous
staircase, although the staircase is only lighted with
ten-watt bulbs and is full of shadows in the evening.
There is not always enough hot water and it is often
drafty, for Rome is sometimes cold and rainy in the winter in spite of all the naked statues. It might make you
angry to hear the men in the dark streets singing melodi-
ously about the roses of eternal spring and the sunny
Mediterranean skies. You could sing a song, I guess,
about the cold *trattorie* and the cold churches, the cold
wine shops and the cold bars, about the burst pipes and
the backfired toilets and about how the city lies under the
snow like an old man with a stroke and everybody
coughing in the streets—even the archdukes and cardinals coughing—but it wouldn't make much of a song. I

go to the Sant' Angelo di Padova International School for Catholics although I am not a Catholic and take communion at Saint Paul within the Gates every Sunday morning. In the wintertime there are usually only two of us in church, not counting the priest or canon, and the other is a man I don't like to sit beside because he smells of Chinese Temple Incense although it has occurred to me that when I have not had a bath for three or four days because of the shortage of hot water in the palace he may not want to sit beside me. When the tourists come in March there are more people in church.

In the beginning most of my mother's friends were Americans and she used to give a big American party at Christmas each year. There was champagne and cake and my mother's friend Tibi would play the piano and they would all stand around the piano and sing "Silent Night" and "We Three Kings of Orient Are" and "Hark the Herald Angels Sing" and other carols from home. I never liked these parties because all the divorcées used to cry. There are hundreds of American divorcées in Rome and they are all friends of my mother's and after the second verse of "Silent Night" they would all begin to bawl, but once I was on the street on Christmas Eve, walking down the street in front of our palace when the windows were open because it was warm or perhaps to let the smoke out from those high windows, and I heard all these people singing "Silent Night" in this foreign city with its ruins and its fountains and it gave me gooseflesh. My mother stopped giving this party when she got to know so many titled Italians. My mother likes the nobility and she doesn't care what they look like. Sometimes the old Princess Tavola-Calda comes to our house for tea. She is either a dwarf or shrunk with age. Her clothes are thin and held together with darns and she always explains that her best clothes, the court dresses and so forth, are in a big trunk but that she has lost the key. She has chin whiskers and a mongrel dog named Zimba on a piece of clothesline. She comes to our house to fill up on tea cakes, but my mother doesn't care because she is a real princess and has the blood of Caesars in her veins.

My mother's best friend is an American writer named Tibi who lives in Rome. There are plenty of these but I don't think they do much writing. Tibi is usually very tired. He wants to go to the opera in Naples but he is too tired to make the trip. Tibi wants to go to the country for a month and finish his novel but all you can get to eat in the country is roast lamb and roast lamb makes Tibi tired. Tibi has never seen the Castel Sant' Angelo because just the thought of walking across the river makes Tibi tired. Tibi is always going here or going there but he never goes anywhere because he is so tired. At first you might think someone should put him into a cold shower or light a firecracker under his chair and then you realize that Tibi really is tired or that this tiredness gets him what he wants out of life such as my mother's affections and that he lies around our palace with a purpose just as I expect to get what I want out of life by walking around the streets as if I had won a prize fight or a tennis match.

That autumn we were planning to drive down to Naples with Tibi and say good-by to some friends who were sailing for home, but Tibi came around to the palace that morning and said he was too *tired* to make the trip. My mother doesn't like to go anywhere without Tibi and first she was gentle with him and said we would all go down together on the train but Tibi was too tired even for this. Then they went into another room and I could hear my mother's voice and when she came out I could see she had been crying and she and I went down to Naples alone on the train. We were going to stay two nights there with an old marquesa and see the ship off and go to the opera at San Carlo. We went down that day and the sailing was the next morning, and we said good-by and watched the lines fall into the water as the ship began to move.

By now the harbor of Naples must be full of tears, so many are wept there whenever a boat pulls out with its load of emigrants, and I wondered what it would feel like to go away once more because you hear so much talk about loving Italy among my mother's friends that you might think the peninsula was shaped more like a naked woman than a boot. Would I miss it, I wondered, or would it all slip away like a house of cards, would it all slip away and be forgotten? Beside me on the wharf was an old Italian lady in black clothes who kept calling across the water, "Blessed are you, blessed are you, you will see the New World," but the man she was shouting to, he was an old, old man, was crying like a baby.

After lunch there was nothing to do so I bought an excursion ticket to Vesuvius. There were some Germans and Swiss on the bus and these two American girls, the one who had dyed her hair in some hotel washbasin a funny shade of red and was wearing a mink stole in spite of the heat and the other who had not dyed her hair at all and at the sight of whom my heart, like a big owl, some night bird anyhow, spread its wings and flew away. She was beautiful. Just looking at her different parts, her nose and her neck and so forth, made her seem more beautiful. She kept poking her fingers into her back hair—patting and poking it—and just watching her do this made me very happy. I was jumping, I was positively jumping just watching her fix her hair. I could see I was making a fool of myself so I looked out of the window at all the smoking chimneys south of Naples and the *Autostrada* there and thought that when I next saw her she would look less beautiful and so I waited until we got to the end of the *Autostrada* and looked again and she was as fair as ever.

They were together and there wasn't any way of getting between them when we lined up for the chair lift but then after we were swung up the mountain to the summit it turned out that the redhead couldn't walk around because she had on sandals and the hot cinders of the volcano burned her feet so I offered to show her friend the sights, what there were to be seen, Sorrento and Capri in the distance and the crater and so forth. Her name was Eva and she was an American making a tour and when I asked her about her friend she said the redhead wasn't her friend at all but that they had just met in the bus and sat down together because they could both speak English but that was all. She told me she was an actress, she was twenty-two years old and did television commercials, mostly advertising ladies' razors, but that she only did the speaking part, some other girl did the shaving and that she had made enough money doing this to come to Europe.

I sat with Eva on the bus back into Naples and we talked all the time. She said she liked Italian cooking and that her father had not wanted her to come alone to Europe. She had quarreled with her father. I told her everything I could think of, even about my father being buried in the Protestant Cemetery. I thought I would ask her to have supper with me at Santa Lucia and so forth but then somewhere near the Garibaldi Station the bus ran into one of those little Fiats and there was the usual thing that happens in Italy when you have a collision. The driver got out to make a speech and everybody got out to hear him and then when we got back into the bus again, Eva wasn't there. It was late in the day and near the station and very crowded, but I've seen enough movies of men looking for their loved ones in railroad-station crowds to feel sure that this was all going to end happily and I looked for her for an hour on the street, but I never saw her again. I went back to the place where we were staying, but there was no one at home, thank God, and I went up to my room, a furnished room—I forgot to say that the marquesa rented rooms—and lay down on my bed and put my face in my arms and thought again that I was never going to get all the loving I needed, no, never.

Later my mother came in and said that I would get my clothes all rumpled, lying around like that. Then she sat down in a chair by my window and asked wasn't the view *divine* although I knew that all she could see was a lagoon and some hills and some fishermen on a wharf. I was cross at my mother and with some reason too because she has always taught me to respect invisible things and I have been an apt pupil but I could see that night that nothing invisible was going to improve the way I felt. She has always taught me that the most powerful moral forces in life are invisible and I have always gone along with her thinking that starlight and rain are what keep the world from flying to pieces. I went along with her up until that moment when it was revealed to me that all her teaching was wrong—it was fainthearted and revolting like the smell of Chinese Temple Incense that comes off that man in church. What did the starlight have to do with my needs? I have often admired my mother, especially in repose, and she is supposed to be beautiful but that night she seemed to me very misled. I sat on the edge of the bed staring at her and thinking how ignorant she was. Then I had a terrible impulse. What I wanted to do was to give her a boot, a swift kick, and I imagined—I let myself imagine the whole awful scene—the look on her face and the way she would straighten her skirt and say that I was an ungrateful son; that I had never appreciated the advantages of my life: Christmas in Kitzbühel, etc. She said something else about the divine view and the charming fishermen and I went to the window to see what she was talking about.

What was so charming about the fishermen? They were dirty, you could be sure, and dishonest and dumb and one of them was probably drunk because he kept taking swigs out of a wine bottle. While they wasted their time at the wharf their wives and their children were probably waiting for them to bring home some money and what was so charming about that? The sky was golden but this was nothing but an illusion of gas and fire, and the water was blue but the harbor there is full of sewage and the many lights on the hill came from the windows of cold and ugly houses where the rooms would smell of *parmigiano* rinds and washing. The light was golden, but then the golden light changed to another color, deeper and rosier, and I wondered where I had seen the color before and I thought I had seen it on the outer petals of those roses that bloom late on the mountains after the hoar frost. Then it paled off, it got so pale that you could see the smoke from the city rising into the air and then through the smoke the evening star turned on, burning like a street light, and I began to count the other stars as they appeared, but very soon they were countless. Then suddenly my mother began to cry and I knew she was crying because she was so lonely in the world and I was very sorry that I had ever wanted to kick her. Then she said why didn't we not go to San Carlo and take the night train to Rome which is what we did and she was happy to see Tibi lying on the sofa when we got back.

While lying in bed that night, thinking about Eva and everything, in that city where you can't hear the rain, I thought I would go home. Nobody in Italy really understood me. If I said good morning to the porter, he wouldn't know what I was saying. If I went out on the balcony and shouted *help* or *fire* or something like that, nobody would understand. I thought I would like to go back to Nantucket where I would be understood and where there would be many girls like Eva walking on the beach. Also it seemed to me that a person should live in his own country; that there is always something a little funny or queer about people who chose to live in another country. Now my mother has many American friends who speak fluent Italian and wear Italian clothes—everything they have is Italian including their husbands sometimes—but to me there always seems to be something a little funny about them as if their stockings were crooked or their underwear showed and I think this is always true about people who choose to live in another country. I wanted to go home. I talked with my mother about it the next day and she said it was out of the question, I couldn't go alone and she didn't know anyone any more. Then I asked if I could go back for the summer and she said she couldn't afford this, she was going to rent a villa at Santa Marinella and then asked if I could get the money myself could I go and she said of course.

I began to look around then for a part-time job and

these are hard to find, but I asked Tibi and he was help-
ful. He isn't much, but he is always kind. He said he
would keep me in mind and then one day when I came
home he asked me if I would like to work for Roncari,
the sight-seeing company, as a guide on Saturdays and
Sundays. This was perfect for me and they tried me out
the next Saturday on the bus that goes to Hadrian's Villa
and Tivoli and the Americans liked me I guess because
I reminded them of home and I went to work on Sunday. The money was fair and the hours fitted in with
my schoolwork and I also thought that the job might
offer me an opportunity to meet some wealthy American
industrialist who would want to take me back to the
United States and teach me all about the steel business,
but I never did. I saw lots of American wanderers though
and I saw, in my course of duty, how great is the hunger
in many Americans who have comfortable and lovely
homes to wander around the world and see its sights.
Sometimes on Saturdays and Sundays when I watched
them piling into the bus it seemed to me that we are a
wandering breed like the nomads. On the trip we first
went out to the villa where they had a half hour to see
the place and take pictures, and then I counted them off
and we drove up the big hill to Tivoli and the Villa
d'Este. They took more pictures and I showed them
where to buy the cheapest post cards and then we would

drive down the Tiburtina past all the new factories there and into Rome. In the wintertime it was dark when we got back to the city and the bus would go around to all the hotels where they were staying or someplace near anyhow. The tourists were always very quiet on the trip back and I think this was because, in their sightseeing bus, they felt the strangeness of Rome swirling around them with its lights and haste and cooking smells, where they had no friends and relations, no business of any kind really but to visit ruins. The last stop was up by the Pincian Gate and it was often windy there in the winter and I would wonder if there was really any substance to life and if it wasn't all like this, really, hungry travelers, some of them with sore feet, looking for dim hotel lights in a city that is not supposed to suffer winter but that suffers plenty, and everybody speaking another language.

I opened a bank account in the Santo Spirito and on Easter vacation I worked full time on the Rome-Florence run.

In this business there are shirt, bladder, and hair stops. A shirt stop is two days where you can get a shirt washed and a hair stop is three days where the ladies can get their hair fixed. I would pick up the passengers on Monday morning and sitting up in front with the driver would tell them the names of the castles and roads and rivers and villages we went by. We stopped at Avezano and Assisi. Perugia was a bladder stop and we got to Florence about seven in the evening. In the morning I would pick up another group who were coming down from Venice. Venice is a hair stop.

When vacation was over I went back to school but about a week after this they called me from Roncari and said that a guide was sick and could I take the Tivoli bus. Then I did something terrible, I made the worst decision I ever made so far. No one was listening and I said I would. I was thinking about Nantucket and going home to a place where I would be understood. I played hooky the next day and when I came home nobody noticed the difference. I thought I would feel guilty, but I didn't feel guilty at all. What I felt was lonely. Then Roncari called again and I skipped another day and then they offered me a steady job and I never went back to school at all. I was making money, but I felt lonely all the time. I had lost all my friends and my place in the world and it seemed to me that my life was nothing but a lie. Then one of the Italian guides complained because I didn't have a license. They were very strict about this and they had to fire me and then I didn't have any place to go. I couldn't go back to school and I couldn't hang around the palace. I'd get up in the morning and take my books—I always carried my books

—and would just bum around the streets or the forum and eat my sandwiches and sometimes go to the movies in the afternoon. Then when it was time for school and soccer practice to be over I would go home where Tibi was usually sitting around with my mother.

Tibi knew all about my playing hooky and I guess his friends at Roncari had told him but he promised not to tell my mother. We had a long talk together one night when my mother was getting dressed to go out. He was saying first how strange it was that I wanted to go home and he didn't want to go home. Tibi doesn't want to go home because he has a difficult family situation. He doesn't get along with his father who is a businessman and he has a stepmother named Verna and he hates Verna. He doesn't ever want to go home. But then he asked me how much money I had saved and I told him I had enough to get home but not to live on or anything or get back and he said he thought he could do something to help me and I trusted him because after all he had got me the job with Roncari.

The next day was Saturday and my mother told me not to make any plans because we were going to pay a visit to the old Princess Tavola-Calda. I said I didn't much want to go but she said I had to go and that was that. We went over there around four, after the siesta. Her palace is in an old part of Rome where the streets turn in on themselves and a run-down quarter too where like in any other run-down quarter they sell second-hand mattresses and old clothes and powders against fleas and bedbugs and cures for itchiness and other thorns in the flesh of the poor. We could tell which palace was hers because the old Princess had her head out of one of the windows and was having a fight with a fat woman who was sweeping the steps with a broom. We stopped at the corner because my mother thought the Princess would not want us to see her having a fight. The Princess wanted the broom and the fat woman said that if she wanted a broom she could buy a broom. She, the fat woman, had worked for the Princess forty-eight years and was paid so miserably that every night she and her husband sat down to a supper of water and air. The Princess came right back at her in spite of her age and frailty and said she had been robbed by the government and that there was nothing but air in her own stomach and that she needed the broom to sweep the *salone*. Then the fat woman said that if she gave her the broom she would give it to her in the squash. Then the Princess got sarcastic and called the fat woman *cara, cara,* and said she had cared for her like a baby for forty-eight years, bringing her lemons when she was sick and that yet she did not have the gentleness to loan her a broom for a moment. Then the fat woman looked up at the Princess and took her right hand and bunched her lips together between her thumb and forefinger and made the loudest raspberry I ever heard. Then the Princess said *Cara, cara, thank you very much my dear, my old and gentle friend,* and went away from the window and came back with a pot of water which she meant to dump on the fat woman, but she missed and only wet the steps. Then the fat woman said *Thank you, your royal highness, thank you, Princess,* and went on sweeping and the Princess slammed the windows and went away.

During all of this some men were going in and out of the palace carrying old automobile tires and loading them onto a truck and I found out later that the whole palace, excepting where the Princess lived, was rented out as a warehouse. To the right of the big door there was a porter's apartment and the porter stopped us and asked us what we wanted. My mother said we wanted to take tea with the Princess and he said we were wasting our time. The Princess was crazy—*matta*—and if we thought she was going to give us something we were mistaken because everything she had belonged to him and his wife who had worked for the Princess forty-eight years without a salary. Then he said he didn't like Americans because we had bombed Frascati and Tivoli and all the rest of it. Finally I pushed him out of the way and we climbed up to the third floor where the

Princess had some rooms. Zimba barked when we rang and she opened the door a crack and then she let us in.

I suppose everyone knows what old Rome is like by now but she needed that broom. First she apologized for her ragged clothes but she said that all her best clothes, the court dresses and so forth, were locked up in this trunk and she had lost the key. She has a fancy way of speaking so that you would be sure to know that she is a Princess or at least some kind of a noble in spite of her rags. She is supposed to be a famous miser and I think this is true because although she sometimes sounds crazy you never lose the feeling that she is cunning and greedy. She thanked us for coming, but she said that she could not offer us any tea or coffee or cake or wine because her life was such a misfortune. The land redistribution projects after the war had drawn all the good peasants away from her farms and she could not find anyone to work her lands. The government taxed her so unmercifully that she could not afford to buy a pinch of tea and all that was left to her was her paintings and while these were worth millions the government claimed that they belonged to the nation and would not let her sell them. Then she said she would like to give me a present, a sea shell that had been given to her by the Emperor of Germany when he came to Rome in 1912 and called on her dear father, the Prince.

She went out of the room and she was gone a long time and when she came back she said alas, she could not give me the shell because it was locked up with her court dresses in the trunk with the lost key. We said good-by and went out, but the porter was waiting for us to make sure we hadn't gotten anything and we walked back home through the terrible traffic and the dark streets.

Tibi was there when we got back and he had dinner with us and then late that night when I was reading someone knocked on my bedroom door and it was Tibi. He seemed to have gone out because he had his coat on over his shoulders like a cloak the way the Romans do. He also had on his plush hat and his tight pants and his plush shoes with gold buckles and he looked like a messenger. I think he felt like a messenger too because he was very excited and spoke to me in a whisper. He said it was all arranged. The old princess had a painting that she wanted to sell in the United States and he had convinced her that I could smuggle it in. It was a small painting, a Pinturicchio, not much bigger than a shirt. All I had to do was to look like a schoolboy and no one would search my bags. He had given the old woman all of his money as security and he said some other people had bought in and I wondered if he meant my mother, but I didn't think this was possible. When I delivered the painting in New York I would be paid five hundred dollars. He would drive me down to Naples on Saturday morning. There was a little airline that carried passengers and freight between Naples and Madrid and I could take this and catch a plane for New York in Madrid and pick up my five hundred dollars on Monday morning. Then he went away. It was after midnight, but I got out of bed and packed my suitcase. I wouldn't be leaving for a week but I was on my way.

I remember the morning I left, Saturday, that is. I got up around seven and had some coffee and looked into my suitcase again. Later I heard the maid taking in my mother's breakfast tray. There was nothing to do but wait for Tibi and I went out onto the balcony to watch for him in the street. I knew he would have to park the car in the *piazzale* and cross the street in front of the palace. Saturday in Rome is like any other day and the street was crowded with traffic and there were crowds on the sidewalk—Romans and pilgrims and members of religious orders and tourists with cameras. It was a nice day and while it is not my place to say that Rome is the most beautiful city in the world I have often thought that with its flat-topped pines and the buildings all the colors of ripening, folded in among the hills like bone and paper, and those big round clouds that in Nantucket would mean a thunderstorm before supper but that mean nothing in Rome, only that the sky will turn purple and fill up with stars and all the lighthearted people make it a lively place to be; and at least a thousand travelers before me, at least a thousand must have said that the light and the air are like wine, those yellow wines from the castelli that you drink in the fall. Then in the crowd I noticed someone wearing the brown habit that they wear at the Sant' Angelo School and then I saw it was my home-room teacher, Father Antonini. He was looking for our address. The bell rang and the maid answered it and I heard the priest ask for my mother. Then the maid went down to my mother's room and I heard my mother go out to the vestibule and say, "Oh, Father Antonini, how nice to see you."

"Peter has been sick?" he asked.

"What made you think so?"

"He hasn't been in school for six weeks."

"Yes," she said, but you could tell that all of her heart wasn't in the lie. It was very upsetting to hear my mother telling this lie; upsetting because I could see that she didn't care about me or whether or not I got an education or anything, that all she wanted was that I should get Tibi's old picture across the border so that he would have some money. "Yes. He's been very sick."

"Could I see him?"

"Oh, no. I've sent him home to the States."

I left the balcony then and went down the *salone* to the hall and down the hall to my room and waited for her there. "You'd better go down and wait for Tibi," she said. "Kiss me good-by and go. Quickly. *Quickly*. I *hate* scenes." If she hated scenes I wondered then why she always made such painful scenes but this was the way we had parted ever since I could remember and I got my suitcase and went out and waited for Tibi in the courtyard.

It was half-past nine or later before he showed up and even before he spoke I could tell what he was going to say. He was too *tired* to drive me to Naples. He had the Pinturicchio wrapped in brown paper and twine and I opened my suitcase and put it in with my shirts. I didn't say good-by to him—I made up my mind then that I was never going to speak to him again—and I started for the station.

I have been to Naples many times but that day I felt very strange. The first thing when I went into the railroad station I thought I was being followed by the porter from the Palazzo Tavola-Calda. I looked around twice but this stranger bent his face over a newspaper and I couldn't be sure but I felt so strange anyhow that it seemed I might have imagined him. Then when I was standing in line at the ticket window someone touched me on the shoulder and I had that awful feeling that my father had come back to give me help. It was an old man who wanted a match and I lighted his cigarette but I could still feel the warmth of the touch on my shoulder and that memory that we would all be happy together again and help one another and then the feeling that I would never get all the loving I needed, no, never.

I got into the train and watched the other passengers hurrying along the platform and this time I saw the porter. There was no mistake. I had only seen him once but I could remember his face and I guessed he was looking for me. He didn't seem to see me and went on down to the third-class compartments and I wondered then if this was the Big World, if this was really what it was like—women throwing themselves away over half-wits like Tibi and purloined paintings and pursuers. I wasn't worried about the porter but I was worried about the idea that life was this much of a contest.

(But I am not a boy in Rome but a grown man in the old prison and river town of Ossining, swatting hornets on this autumn afternoon with a rolled-up newspaper. I can see the Hudson River from my window. A dead rat floats downstream and two men in a sinking rowboat come up against the tide. One of them is rowing desperately with a boat seat and I wonder have they escaped from prison or have they just been fishing for perch and why should I exchange this scene for the dark streets around the Pantheon? Why, never having received from my parents anything but affection and understanding, should I invent a grotesque old man, a foreign grave and a foolish mother? What is the incurable loneliness that makes me want to pose as a fatherless child in a cold wind and wouldn't the imposture make a better story than Tibi and the Pinturicchio? But my father taught me, while we hoed the beans, that I should complete for better or for worse whatever I had begun and so we go back to the scene where he leaves the train in Naples.)

In Naples I got off the train at the Margellina hoping to duck the porter. Only a handful of people got off there and I don't think the porter was one of them although I couldn't be sure. There was a little hotel on a side street near the station and I went there and took a room and left my suitcase with the painting in it under the bed and locked the door. Then I went out to look for the office of the airline where I could buy my ticket and this was way on the other side of Naples. It was a small airline and a very small office and I think the man who sold me my ticket was probably the pilot too. The plane left at eleven that night so then I walked back to the hotel and as soon as I stepped into the lobby the lady at the desk said that my friend was waiting for me and there he was, the porter, with two *carabinieri*. He began to holler and yell—all the same things. I had bombed Frascati and Tivoli and invented the hydrogen bomb and now I was stealing one of the paintings that formed the invaluable heritage of the Italian people. The *carabinieri* were really very nice although I don't like to talk with people who wear swords but when I asked if I could call the consulate they said yes and I did. It was about four o'clock then and they said they would send an officer over and pretty soon this big nice American came over who kept saying, "Yurp." I told him I was carrying a package for a friend and that I didn't know what it contained and he said, "Yurp, yurp." He had on a big double-breasted suit and he seemed to be having some trouble with his belt or his underwear because every so often he would take hold of his waist and give it a big yank. Then everyone agreed that in order to open my package they would have to get a justice and I got my bag and we all got into the car the consular officer had and drove off to some *questura* or courthouse where we had to wait a half hour for the justice to put on his sash of office with the golden fringe. Then I opened my suitcase and he passed the package to an attendant who undid the knots in the twine. Then the justice unwrapped the package and there was nothing in it but a piece of cardboard. The porter let out such a roar of anger and disappointment when he saw this that I don't think he could have been an àccomplice and I think the old lady must have thought the whole thing up herself. They would never get back the money they had paid her, any of them, and I could see her, licking her chops like Reddy the Fox. I even felt sorry for Tibi.

In the morning I tried to get a refund on my plane ticket but the office was shut and so then I walked to the Margellina to get the morning train to Rome. A ship was in. There were twenty-five or thirty tourists waiting on the platform. They were tired and excited, you could see, and were pointing at the espresso machine and asking if they couldn't have a large cup with cream but they didn't seem funny to me that morning—they seemed to be nice and admirable and it seemed to me that there was a lot of seriousness at the bottom of their wandering. I was not as disappointed myself as I have been about less important things and I even felt a little cheerful because I knew that I would go back to Nantucket sometime or if not to Nantucket to some place where I would be understood. And then I remembered that old lady in Naples, so long ago, shouting across the water, "Blessed are you, blessed are you, you will see America, you will see the New World," and I knew that large cars and frozen food and hot water were not what she meant.

"Blessed are you, blessed are you," she kept shouting across the water and I knew that she thought of a place where there are no police with swords and no greedy nobility and no dishonesty and no briberies and no delays and no fear of cold and hunger and war and if all that she imagined was not true, it was a noble idea and that was the main thing.

A MISCELLANY OF
CHARACTERS THAT WILL
NOT APPEAR

1. THE PRETTY GIRL AT THE PRINCETON-DARTmouth Rugby game. She wandered up and down behind the crowd that was ranged along the foul line. She seemed to have no date, no particular companion but to be known to everyone. Everyone called her name (Florrie), everyone was happy to see her, and, as she stopped to speak with friends, one man put his hand flat on the small of her back, and at this touch (in spite of the fine weather and the green of the playing field) a dark and thoughtful look came over his face, as if he felt immortal longings. Her hair was a fine dark gold, and she pulled a curl down over her eyes and peered through it. Her nose was a little too quick, but the effect was sensual and aristocratic, her arms and legs were round and fine but not at all womanly, and she squinted her violet eyes. It was the first half, there was no score, and Dartmouth kicked the ball offside. It was a muffed kick, and it went directly into her arms. The catch was graceful; she seemed to have been chosen to receive the ball and stood there for a second, smiling, bowing, observed by everyone, before she tossed it charmingly and clumsily back into play. There was some applause. Then everyone turned their attention from Florrie back to the field, and a second later she dropped to her knees, covered her face with her hands, recoiling violently from the excitement. She seemed very shy. Someone opened a can of beer and passed it to her, and she stood and wandered again along the foul line and out of the pages of my novel because I never saw her again.

2. All parts for Marlon Brando.

3. All scornful descriptions of American landscapes with ruined tenements, automobile dumps, polluted rivers, jerry-built ranch houses, abandoned miniature golf links, cinder deserts, ugly hoardings, unsightly oil

derricks, diseased elm trees, eroded farmlands, gaudy and fanciful gas stations, unclean motels, candle-lit tea-rooms, and streams paved with beer cans, for these are not, as they might seem to be, the ruins of our civilization but are the temporary encampments and outposts of the civilization that we—you and I—shall build.

4. All such scenes as the following: "Clarissa stepped into the room and then —————————————————— ——————————————————." Out with this and all other explicit descriptions of sexual commerce, for how can we describe the most exalted experience of our physical lives, as if—jack, wrench, hubcap, and nuts —we were describing the changing of a flat tire?

5. All lushes. For example: The curtain rises on the copy office of a Madison Avenue advertising agency, where X, our principal character, is working out the exploitation plans for a new brand of rye whiskey. On a drafting table to the right of his fruitwood desk is a pile of suggestions from the art department. Monarchal and baronial crests and escutcheons have been suggested for the label. For advertising there is a suggested scene of plantation life where the long-gone cotton aristocracy drink whiskey on a magnificent porch. X is not satisfied with this and examines next a water color of pioneer America. How fresh, cold, and musical is the stream that pours through the forest. The tongues of the brook speak

into the melancholy silence of a lost wilderness, and what is that in the corner of the blue sky but a flight of carrier pigeons. On a rock in the foreground a wiry young man, in rude leather clothing and a coonskin hat, is drinking rye from a stone jug. This prospect seems to sadden X, and he goes on to the next suggestion, which is that one entertain with rye; that one invite to one's house one exploded literary celebrity, one unemployed actress, the grandniece of a president of the United States, one broken-down bore, and one sullen and wicked literary critic. They stand grouped around an enormous bottle of rye. This picture disgusts X, and he goes on to the last, where a fair young couple in evening dress stand at dusk on a medieval battlement (aren't those the lights and towers of Siena in the distance?) toasting what must be a seduction of indescribable prowess and duration in the rye that is easy on your dollar.

X is not satisfied. He turns away from the drafting table and walks toward his desk. He is a slender man of undiscernible age, although time seems to have seized upon his eye sockets and the scruff of his neck. This last is seamed and scored as wildly as some disjointed geodetic survey. There is a cut as deep as a saber scar running diagonally from the left to the right of his neck with so many deep and numerous branches and tributaries that the effect is discouraging. But it is in his eyes that the recoil of time is most noticeable. Here we see, as on a sandy point we see the working of two tides, how the powers of his exaltation and his misery, his lusts and his aspirations, have stamped a wilderness of wrinkles onto the dark and pouchy skin. He may have tired his eyes looking at Vega through a telescope or reading Keats by a dim light, but his gaze seems hangdog and impure. These details would lead you to believe that he was a man of some age, but suddenly he drops his left shoulder very gracefully and shoots the cuff of his silk shirt as if he were eighteen—nineteen at the most. He glances at his Italian calendar watch. It is ten in the morning. His office is soundproofed and preternaturally still. The voice of the city comes faintly to his high window. He stares at his dispatch case, darkened by the rains of England, France, Italy, and Spain. He is in the throes of a grueling melancholy that makes the painted walls of his office (pale yellow and pale blue) seem like fabrications of paper put up to conceal the volcanos and floodwaters that are the terms of his misery. He seems to be approaching the moment of his death, the moment of his conception, some critical point in time. His head, his shoulders, and his hands begin to tremble. He opens his dispatch case, takes out a bottle of rye, gets to his knees, and thirstily empties the bottle.

167

He is on the skids, of course, and we will bother with only one more scene. After having been fired from the office where we last saw him he is offered a job in Cleveland, where the rumors of his weakness seem not to have reached. He has gone to Cleveland to settle the arrangements and rent a house for his family. Now they are waiting at the railroad station for him to return with good news. His pretty wife, his three children, and the two dogs have all come down to welcome Daddy. It is dusk in the suburb where they live. They are, by this time, a family that have received more than their share of discouragements, but in having been recently denied the common promises and rewards of their way of life —the new car and the new bicycle—they have discovered a melancholy but steady quality of affection that has nothing to do with acquisitions. They have glimpsed, in their troubled love for Daddy, the thrill of a destiny. The local rattles into view. A soft spray of golden sparks falls from the brake box as the train slows and halts. They all feel, in the intensity of their anticipation, nearly incorporeal. Seven men and two women leave the train, but where is Daddy? It takes two conductors to get him down the stairs. He has lost his hat, his necktie, and his topcoat, and someone has blacked his right eye. He still holds the dispatch case under one arm. No one speaks, no one weeps as they get him into the car and drive him out of our sight, out of our jurisdiction and concern. Out they go, male and female, all the lushes; they throw so little true light on the way we live.

6. And while we are about it, out go all those homosexuals who have taken such a dominating position in recent fiction. Isn't it time that we embraced the indiscretion and inconstancy of the flesh and moved on? The scene this time is Hewitt's Beach on the afternoon of the Fourth of July. Mrs. Ditmar, the wife of the governor, and her son Randall have carried their picnic lunch up the beach to a deserted cove, although the American flag on the clubhouse can be seen flying beyond the dunes. The boy is sixteen, well formed, his skin the fine gold of youth, and he seems to his lonely mother so beautiful that she admires him with trepidation. For the last ten years her husband, the governor, has neglected her in favor of his intelligent and pretty executive secretary. Mrs. Ditmar has absorbed, with the extraordinary commodiousness of human nature, a nearly daily score of wounds. Of course she loves her son. She finds nothing of her husband in his appearance. He has the best qualities of *her* family, she thinks, and she is old enough to think that such things as a slender foot and fine hair are marks of breeding, as indeed they may be. His shoulders are square. His body is compact. As he throws a stone into the sea, it is not the force with which

he throws the stone that absorbs her but the fine grace with which his arm completes the circular motion once the stone has left his hand—as if every gesture he made were linked, one to the other. Like any lover, she is immoderate and does not want the afternoon with him to end. She does not dare wish for an eternity, but she wishes the day had more hours than is possible. She fingers her pearls in her worn hands, and admires their sea lights, and wonders how they would look against his golden skin.

He is a little bored. He would rather be with men and girls his own age, but his mother has supported him and defended him so he finds some security in her company. She has been a stanch and formidable protector. She can and has intimidated the headmaster and most of the teachers at his school. Offshore he sees the sails of the racing fleet and wishes briefly that he were with them, but he refused an invitation to crew and has not enough self-confidence to skipper, so in a sense he chose to be alone on the beach with his mother. He is timid about competitive sports, about the whole appearance of organized society, as if it concealed a force that might tear him to pieces; but why is this? Is he a coward, and is there such a thing? Is one born a coward, as one is born dark or fair? Is his mother's surveillance excessive; has she gone so far in protecting him that he has become vulnerable and morbid? But considering how intimately he knows the depth of her unhappiness, how can he forsake her until she has found other friends?

He thinks of his father with pain. He has tried to know and love his father, but all their plans come to nothing. The fishing trip was canceled by the unexpected arrival of the governor of Massachusetts. At the ballpark a messenger brought him a note saying that his father would be unable to come. When he fell out of the pear tree and broke his arm, his father would undoubtedly have visited him in the hospital had he not been in Washington. He learned to cast with a fly rod, feeling that, cast by cast, he might work his way into the terrain of his father's affection and esteem, but his father had never found time to admire him. He can grasp the urgency of his father's tasks, but he cannot grasp the power of his own disappointment. This emotion surrounds him like a mass of energy, but an energy that has no wheels to drive, no stones to move. These sad thoughts can be seen in his posture. His shoulders droop. He looks childish and forlorn, and his mother calls him to her.

He sits in the sand at her feet, and she runs her fingers through his light hair. Then she does something hideous. One wants to look away but not before we have seen her undo her pearls and fasten them around his golden neck. "See how they shine," says she, doing the clasp as irrevocably as the manacle is welded to the prisoner's shin.

Out they go; out they go; for, like Clarissa and the lush, they shed too little light.

7. In closing—in closing, that is, for this afternoon (I have to go to the dentist and then have my hair cut), I would like to consider the career of my laconic old friend Royden Blake. We can, for reasons of convenience, divide his work into four periods. First there were the bitter moral anecdotes—he must have written a hundred—that proved that most of our deeds are sinful. This was followed, as you will remember, by nearly a decade of snobbism, in which he never wrote of characters who had less than sixty-five thousand dollars a year. He memorized the names of the Groton faculty and the bartenders at "21." All of his characters were waited on hand and foot by punctilious servants, but when you went to his house for dinner you found the chairs held together with picture wire, you ate fried eggs from a cracked plate, the doorknobs came off in your hand, and if you wanted to flush the toilet you had to lift the lid off the water tank, roll up a sleeve, and reach deep into the cold and rusty water to manipulate the valves. When he had finished with snobbism, he made the error I have mentioned in Item 4 and then moved on into his ro-

mantic period, where he wrote "The Necklace of Malvio D'Alfi" (with that memorable scene of childbirth on a mountain pass), "The Wreck of the S.S. *Lorelei*," "The King of the Trojans," and "The Lost Girdle of Venus," to name only a few. He was quite sick at the time, and his incompetence seemed to be increasing. His work was characterized by everything that I have mentioned. In his pages one found alcoholics, scarifying descriptions of the American landscape, and fat parts for Marlon Brando. You might say that he had lost the gift of evoking the perfumes of life: sea water, the smoke of burning hemlock, and the breasts of women. He had damaged, you might say, the ear's innermost chamber, where we hear the heavy noise of the dragon's tail moving over the dead leaves. I never liked him, but he was a colleague and a drinking companion, and when I heard, in my home in Kitzbühel, that he was dying, I drove to Innsbruck and took the express to Venice, where he then lived. It was in the late autumn. Cold and brilliant. The boarded-up palaces of the Grand Canal—gaunt, bedizened, and crowned—looked like the haggard faces of that grade of nobility that shows up for the royal weddings in Hesse. He was living in a *pensione* on a back canal. There was a high tide, the reception hall was flooded, and I got to the staircase over an arrangement of duckboards. I brought him a bottle of Turinese gin and a package of Austrian cigarettes, but he was too far gone for these, I saw when I sat down in a painted chair (broken) beside his bed. "I'm working," he exclaimed. "I'm working. I can see it all. Listen to me!"

"Yes," I said.

"It begins like this," he said, and changed the level of his voice to correspond, I suppose, to the gravity of his narrative. "The Transalpini stops at Kirchbach at midnight," he said, looking in my direction to make sure that I had received the full impact of this poetic fact.

"Yes," I said.

"Here the passengers for Vienna continue on," he said sonorously, "while those for Padua must wait an hour. The station is kept open and heated for their convenience, and there is a bar where one may buy coffee and wine. One snowy night in March, three strangers at this bar fell into a conversation. The first was a tall, bald-headed man, wearing a sable-lined coat that reached to his ankles. The second was a beautiful American woman going to Isvia to attend funeral services for her only son, who had been killed in a mountain-climbing accident. The third was a white-haired, heavy Italian woman in a black shawl, who was treated with great deference by the waiter. He bowed from the waist when he poured her a glass of cheap wine, and addressed her as 'Your Majesty.' Avalanche warnings had been posted earlier in the day. . . ." Then he put his head back on the pillow and died—indeed, these were his dying words, and the dying words, it seemed to me, of generations of storytellers, for how could this snowy and trumped-up pass, with its trio of travelers, hope to celebrate a world that lies spread out around us like a bewildering and stupendous dream?

About the Author

John Cheever was born in Quincy, Massachusetts, in 1912. His first story was published when he was sixteen.

Since then Mr. Cheever has gained a distinguished reputation as a short-story writer. Over a hundred of his stories have been published, chiefly in *The New Yorker*. One of these stories, "The Enormous Radio," is perhaps the most widely anthologized short story of the decade. Three collections of Mr. Cheever's stories have appeared: *The Way Some People Live* (1943), *The Enormous Radio* (1953), and *The Housebreaker of Shady Hill* (1958).

Mr. Cheever was awarded a Guggenheim Fellowship in 1951 and in 1956 he received the National Institute of Arts and Letters award in literature. *The Wapshot Chronicle,* Mr. Cheever's first novel, won the National Book Award for fiction in 1957.

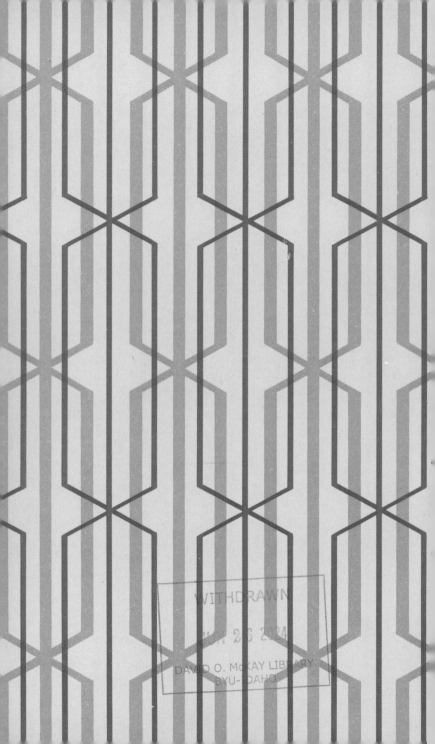